A GRIM ENDING

Rachel Stanley

Stanley Publications

Copyright © 2022 Rachel Stanley
All rights reserved.
ISBN: 978-1-8380272-5-4

For my mum, Margaret Eyre. Hopefully when you read A Grim Ending, you'll understand why I've dedicated this, rather than any of my other books, to you.

BOOKS BY RACHEL STANLEY

A Grim Series
A Grim Affair (Book One)
A Grim Haunt (Book Two)
A Grim Ending (Book Three)

CONTENTS

	Acknowledgements	I
	Prologue	Pg 1
1	Chapter 1 – Ellie	Pg 4
2	Chapter 2 – Emma	Pg 11
3	Chapter 3 – Emma	Pg 21
4	Chapter 4 – Blake	Pg 33
5	Chapter 5 – Emma	Pg 36
6	Chapter 6 – Blake	Pg 46
7	Chapter 7 – Ellie	Pg 49
8	Chapter 8 – Ellie	Pg 56
9	Chapter 9 – Emma	Pg 62
10	Chapter 10 – Blake	Pg 73
11	Chapter 11 – Ellie	Pg 76
12	Chapter 12 – Blake	Pg 86
13	Chapter 13 – Emma	Pg 90
14	Chapter 14 – Emma	Pg 98
15	Chapter 15 – Ellie	Pg 105
16	Chapter 16 – Ellie	Pg 110
17	Chapter 17 – Emma	Pg 116
18	Chapter 18 – Ellie	Pg 122
19	Chapter 19 – Emma	Pg 133
20	Chapter 20 – Blake	Pg 143
21	Chapter 21 – Ellie	Pg 148
22	Chapter 22 – Ellie	Pg 156
23	Chapter 23 – Emma	Pg 161
24	Chapter 24 – Emma	Pg 168
25	Chapter 25 – Blake	Pg 175
	Epilogue	Pg 177

ACKNOWLEDGEMENTS

I can't believe I've finally done it; I've finally finished *A Grim Series*. I started writing *A Grim Affair* as a way to unwind after work because, while I love my day job, it can be a little busy at times. And now, almost six years later, Emma's story is complete. It's been tough at times—this book in particular has been hard to write—and I don't know if I'd have found the strength to finish if it hadn't been for you. And I do mean you reading this. So, first of all, I want to say a huge thank you to every single one of you who's read *A Grim Affair* and *A Grim Haunt* and who's enjoyed both enough to want to find out how Emma's story ends. I hope you're happy when you get to the end of *A Grim Ending*. If not, all I can say is that I truly believe this is how it had to be.

Of course, and as always, I'm also extremely grateful to my wonderfully supportive family and some fabulous friends: my mum, Margaret Eyre; my brother, Daniel, and his family, Jessica, Ewan, and Esme Eyre; my in-laws, Joan and Peter Stanley; my brother-in-law, Phil Stanley; and one of my best friends, Jessica Cantwell. Mum, I hope you enjoy reading all three books one after the other now that they're all out, and Jessica, thank you for reading and re-reading *A Grim Ending* until I got it right.

Lastly, there are three in my life who make me feel like I'm the luckiest girl alive. My husband, David Stanley, and my furbabies, Cooper and Watson. My poor husband has to listen to me witter on about plot points on a very regular basis, never mind the fact that he has next to no interest in supernatural romantic thrillers! And both Cooper and Watson, who are drawn to the laptop in much the same way that a moth is drawn to a flame, routinely have to put up with me typing around them. It's no way to have cuddles really, is it?

As with both *A Grim Affair* and *A Grim Haunt*, the very first version of *A Grim Ending* wasn't quite right. I knew that, of course I did, but I couldn't quite put my finger on what was wrong with it. That's when my beta readers rode into view on their shining white horses.

Mum, Dave, and Jessica, with the help of Donna White, Kirsten Flores, Steven Mills, and Kimberley Quay all helped to refine *A Grim Ending* into the version that you hold in your hands or have downloaded onto your kindles.

There are just a couple more people that I need to thank: Beck Michaels for designing the cover (which I'm sure you'll agree is absolutely stunning, although there is now a debate happening as to which is the best of the covers!) and Lee Munro for completing the final read through.

My thanks to you all.

P.S. As with both *A Grim Affair* and *A Grim Haunt*, any mistakes that you find in *A Grim Ending* are all my own. The final say was always mine after all. If you find a typo, though, feel free to let me know.

P.P.S. Can I just remind you all that I am an English writer and, as a consequence, all of my books are edited in U.K. English, not American English? In *A Grim Ending*, more than in *A Grim Affair* or *A Grim Haunt*, my American beta readers commented on some of the slang, that's all.

Prologue
Sunday 22nd November 1914

The crude, wooden structure had been Edward's home for longer than he cared to remember. It was nothing like his actual home. In fact, it could barely be called a dwelling, but it *was* where he rested his head whenever he had the chance. It had been dug into the trench walls, offering him a somewhat private retreat from the horrors of war, as was befitting of his station. To call it private, though, was really overstating it; it only had three walls. The front had simply been left open to the elements. Still, it was pure luxury compared to what his men had to suffer; at least he had somewhere that was his and his alone. Not only that, but timber buttresses held up a corrugated iron roof, which kept the rain out; he had a hay bale on which he could lie flat; *and* he had a simple wooden chair to sit on.

The onset of winter had forced a break in the hostilities, and so Edward was taking the opportunity to relax for a while. He'd leant back on his chair and propped his feet up, using the hay bale as a footstool. With his eyes closed, he could almost believe that he was back in England. Unfortunately, with them open, he had no choice but to accept that he was not. From where he was sitting, he could see one of his men squeezing himself deeper and deeper into a crevice that had been dug into the trench wall. George something or other, he thought. He'd stopped worrying about their names after only a few days on the front because they all had a nasty habit of dying on him. If they weren't shot dead by the enemy, trench foot got them.

George's misery was written all over his face. With the exception of his cheeks, which were a rosy red colour, his skin had turned translucent, and he was shivering so hard that Edward briefly thought about inviting him into his dugout. Only briefly, mind you. He didn't really want to share his little sanctuary with anyone else. No, he was happy on his own. Not that anyone could claim to be happy grubbing about in what was essentially a muddy hole, but at least his feet were warm and dry courtesy of a pair of stout knee-length boots and some thick woollen socks.

No doubt the demons would be dismayed that his misery had been stemmed for the moment. They revelled in desolation. Not just in his, of course. They adored the agony of misfortune. The fact that dead bodies littered no-man's-land would have them clapping their hands together in gleeful delight, and while he had killed and would no doubt kill again, the atrocities of war had started to turn his stomach.

Edward had grown up in a world of demons, you see. His family had formed an alliance with them generations previously, but he didn't know why. All he knew was that he was expected to follow orders regardless of if those orders came from his father, an uncle, or one of the demons. Not that he was allowed to interact with the demons all that much, at only twenty-eight, he was considered too young still. One day he would find out more, once the accursed war was over perhaps, but until then, he was left to piece together whatever he could.

He'd already discovered that they were searching for someone. Someone who had to meet with 'the Key' for some reason. The Key was a young woman named Maggie; they knew pretty much everything there was to know about her. In fact, several members of his extended family were acquainted with her. He wasn't, he'd only ever been allowed to catch brief glimpses of her, but she looked to be about his age with striking copper-coloured hair. Personally, he didn't get their fascination with her, he preferred blondes, but she was all they talked about. Her every move was watched and catalogued. He didn't think she knew that she was the star of their show though.

Who they were looking for remained a mystery. He knew that they were searching for a man, but they never talked about him by name. They only ever said 'he,' and he (whoever he was!) didn't seem to have a title in the same way that Maggie was reverently referred to as the Key.

Edward was hoping that it would all be made clear when he finally went through his initiation, assuming that he was allowed to go through it. Only a select few were chosen. He'd heard rumours about what the ceremony entailed, but he assumed most were embellished. Some said that he'd have to drink demon blood, while others assured him that he'd have to sign away his soul. He'd scoffed at the idea of both, but either way, he didn't care what he had to do. He'd do whatever it took to learn the family secrets. After all, his father was the head of the family; it was only right and proper that he took over, assuming he survived the bloody war, of course.

Chapter 1 – Ellie
Monday 27th May 2019

Ellie wandered aimlessly about in the bright white landscape. Everything about it was white, even the clothes that she wore—a pair of linen trousers, a scoop neck T-shirt, and a loosely fitted overshirt. From what she could see, there were no edges in the place that she'd woken up in; no floor, no sky, no nothing. It was just an endless… void. That was the only word she could think of to describe it.

She walked, placing one foot slowly in front of the other, heading in an unknown direction, because she'd been walking when she'd come to her senses. She wasn't frightened or panicked, even though the thought occurred that perhaps she should be. Her emotions seemed to have been switched off somehow. *I'm dreaming,* she thought. *That's the only explanation for what's happening, for why—*

"Eleanor Chapman-Bell," someone interrupted Ellie's idle musings. The voice came from everywhere and nowhere all at the same time, but Ellie didn't flinch or falter at the sound (or even at the use of her full name). She stopped walking and turned in a circle, looking for whoever had spoken, but there was no one there. "Behold what will be if your courage fails you," the voice continued. "Watch what will happen if you do not fulfil your destiny."

With that, Ellie's surroundings changed. The void blurred and dimmed before reforming around her. Ellie's stomach dropped in the same way that it did when she was on a fairground ride. Without thinking, she reached out to steady herself and touched something solid. A wall? What else could it be? It was as smooth as glass though.

It took Ellie's eyes a while to adjust, but eventually she could see well enough to turn around. She was standing in what looked like an underground chamber or cellar. The walls had been polished until they gleamed in the weak light, but the floor was rough concrete.

Ellie glanced first to the left and then to the right, searching for some kind of lamp or torch, but there weren't any. *Odd,* she thought, feeling only intrigued. Her emotions continued to be out of reach, almost as if she were in some kind of trance. All she felt was… nothing. Well, almost nothing. She was mildly curious about what was going on.

At one end of the cellar, stone steps climbed up towards an opening, and at the other, an altar had been erected. A dark red cloth had been draped over a table, the fabric puddling on the floor, and on top of that, a narrow black runner ran end-to-end down the centre of the table. Six or seven unlit candles had then been dotted around. Ellie couldn't help but wonder about the purpose of the altar, but a muffled shout from somewhere above jerked her from her thoughts before she had time to reach any conclusions.

The sound of footsteps rang out in the cellar. Ellie glanced towards the stone steps thinking that she really should hide, but for some reason, she couldn't be bothered. She watched as two men descended from above. She expected them to kick up a fuss about her being there, but they didn't seem to notice her. Or if they did, they ignored her. They made a beeline for the altar, where they repositioned the candles, placing them neatly into two groups before lighting each one in turn.

In time, more men joined the first two until eventually the space felt crowded. All of them were dressed the same, in a black suit, with a black shirt and tie, and a mask covering their faces.

The masks were hideous, depicting the devil and his following of demons. Most were dark in colour—black, charcoal, burgundy, or navy blue—and all were grotesque. Some had horns that pointed straight upwards, while others had horns that curled in vicious-looking spirals. Some had been decorated with strange symbols, while others had been left plain. There wasn't anything about them that was bright or colourful, there wasn't a single feather or bell in sight, nor was there any golden-coloured brocade.

Ellie was still inspecting the men when the buzz of conversation died away. Without prompting, everyone, including Ellie, turned to face the stairwell. Emma, Ellie's very best friend in all the world, was being forcibly dragged into the chamber, and for the first time since waking up in the strange void, Ellie felt a wisp of fear thread its way around her heart.

Emma was clearly distressed; she was obviously being forced to act against her will, and she had no chance of putting up a fight because her hands were tied behind her back. However, she still looked absolutely stunning. Her beauty was astounding. She wasn't slim or petite, instead she was luscious, ripe, a goddess among men.

In stark comparison to Ellie's all-white attire, Emma was dressed all in black. She had on a leather bustier that dipped low at the front, revealing her ample cleavage. It was held in place by two sets of shoe-string straps, the first of which rested on her shoulders while the second set formed a halter neck. The top was split open from just underneath Emma's bust, revealing the creamy-white skin of her stomach. It flared outwards, skimming over the waistband of the floor-length skirt that she wore.

Ellie gasped as Emma was pulled further into the room and pushed to the floor in front of the altar.

"Call him here!" The man who'd dragged Emma into the room barked. He was the only one of the group not wearing a mask. His face was lined with wrinkles, and his dark, hooded eyes were bloodshot, giving him a ghastly appearance.

"Never!" Emma declared while Ellie tried to push her way through the crowd towards her best friend. The men continued to act as if she didn't exist. Either they couldn't perceive her, or they didn't care that she was there. "I won't allow you to use him in this way," Emma continued, her chin held high despite her lowly position.

"If you won't call your beloved boyfriend here of your own free will, we'll let your pain speak for you," the same man snarled. He crouched beside Emma and took hold of her chin, forcing her to face him. "Such a pretty face," he crooned. Emma yanked herself free of his hold, but he didn't seem to notice. "It would be a shame if it got damaged in all of this…" his words trailed off, but he gestured around himself at the goings on.

"I will never let Blake be used by you." Emma spat the words out through clenched teeth. She'd always been stubborn.

The man just laughed as he stood, and with a smirk, he raised his foot high into the air and stamped it down onto Emma's knee. Ellie heard an ominous crack as something shattered.

By some quirk of the dream state, Ellie felt the pain that bloomed in Emma's body. She stumbled as it ripped through her. It felt like someone had stabbed a red-hot poker into the top of her patella. The agony was beyond anything that she'd ever known before. Each ligament snapped independently of the others and, as each one pinged apart inside of her body, waves of sickness washed over her. Sweat glistened on her forehead and trickled down her back, but she didn't realise how clammy she'd gotten, lost as she was in the events that were unfolding around her and the pain that she felt.

Emma fared no better than Ellie, but there was nothing that she could do other than cry out in pain. And then Blake was with her, appearing from nowhere, cradling her in his arms.

"No, Blake, go away," Emma sniffled, but the words were scarcely audible.

"Welcome to the party," the man who'd stamped on Emma's knee said, a chilling, serpentine smile on his face. "Now, let us begin," he continued. He lifted his arms to the ceiling and raised his voice. "Brothers, it is time."

With that, those who were gathered began chanting. Ellie had never heard anything like it before. The words were guttural and harsh. At first, the incantation was softly spoken, but gradually it swelled and grew until, at the crescendo, a new noise could be heard. As Ellie watched, unable to look away, the scaly, clawed hand of a demon reached out from inside of Blake. It ripped apart the skin of Blake's stomach and pushed his ribs wide open while forcing its way into the world. Ellie felt herself starting to heave.

"He may be the Keeper of Souls, but he's also a portal to the other dimensions," the voice that Ellie had heard earlier on whispered softly in her ear. "You have to stop this from happening. You have to kill the Key." And with that, Ellie jerked fully awake, sitting bolt upright in bed. Sweat had plastered her hair to her head and soaked her pyjamas through. After only a moment, she fell back onto her pillow with a plop. Tears leaked from the corners of her eyes, but she didn't bother to brush them away, letting them trail down the side of her face before soaking into her hair.

Some time later, despite the fact that dawn had barely broken, Ellie slid out from underneath the covers, being careful not to disturb Scott. She grabbed her dressing gown and crept from the bedroom, closing the door softly behind her. There was no way that she was going to go back to sleep, not while the memory of her dream was still so fresh in her mind. She tiptoed out into the open-plan living space of her new home, smiling faintly at the thought. Her new home! She'd just spent her very first night in her own place, snuggled up with Scott. She'd never lived on her own before. She'd never even wanted to move out of her mum and dad's. She'd had a spacious bedroom and had gotten on well with both of her parents—that is, until her mum had tried to kill Emma, in this very apartment, in fact.

Ellie glanced towards where it had happened and shuddered. She saw again the glint of the syringe as she'd snatched it from her mum's hand. She glimpsed the look of anguish on her mum's face and the fleeting look of confusion that had crossed Emma's. And of course, she recalled Blake's infernal wrath and how he'd been all for terminating Joanne's life. Anyone who threatened Emma was not only gambling with their life; they were also putting their soul on the line because Blake had the power to be judge, jury, executioner, *and* soul collector. She'd not wanted her mum's death, though, and thankfully neither had Emma. Today they were going to wash away that particular memory with some bright paint and some new furniture.

While wrapping her dressing gown around her and securing it in place with the belt, Ellie drifted into the kitchen, stepping around the boxes that still needed to be unpacked. They contained everything that she needed to transform the apartment into her home. Idly, she wondered what had possessed her to accept her mum's proposition. They'd formed a wary truce in recent weeks, but each of them was always on edge. When her dad had started to ask questions, her mum had suggested she move out, seeing as there was a fully (albeit sparsely) furnished place ready and waiting. All Ellie had to do was say yes. And why wouldn't she, other than the fact that the apartment held mostly bad memories? In the end, she'd acquiesced just to get away from her mum. She'd resolved to make new memories, and she was excited to get started. At least, that's what she was telling herself.

Ellie flicked the kettle on to boil before going to stand at one of the picture windows that overlooked the River Ribble. In the early morning light, she could scarcely see the water, but she wasn't really looking at the view anyway. She was thinking about the dream that she'd had. The nightmare. No matter how hard she tried to push them away, images of Emma contorted in agony stubbornly remained at the forefront of her mind. Her own knee suddenly bothered her, so she bent down to rub it. She knew that it had just been a dream, but the pain persisted, albeit as a dull ache rather than the sharp stabbing pain from before. "For goodness sake, Ellie, stop it!" she muttered to herself, standing up straight again.

"Stop what?" Scott asked from behind her, making her jump.

"Scott!"

"Were you expecting someone else?"

"No, of course not, I just… erm…" Ellie's voice trailed off into nothing. She didn't want to tell Scott what was bothering her because she didn't want to relive it, and she couldn't share her fears with him anyway because he was ignorant of the world around him. It wasn't his fault of course; he didn't live in a world of angels and demons, nor did he know that his sister was soulmates with the Grim Reaper, a mostly incorporeal being who'd been in existence for almost a thousand years. He'd yet to be apprised of the fact that Blake, whose preferred title was the Keeper of Souls, attended to the dying on a daily (if not on a minute-by-minute) basis. Not only that, but he was also a portal to the other dimensions—Heaven and Hell.

"You're up early," Scott remarked, casually leaning against the doorframe that separated the living room from the bedroom, seemingly oblivious to the turmoil that raged within Ellie. "Why don't you come back to bed for a bit?" He smiled, his eyes sparkling mischievously in the early morning light.

"I erm… I just… I don't…" Scott was bare-chested and standing in only a pair of grey drawstring pyjama bottoms, but Ellie couldn't quite shake the aftereffects of her dream.

"Hey, what's wrong?" Scott reached up with one hand to rub the sleep from his eyes. He seemed to have only just realised that Ellie was distressed. "We don't have to go back to bed. What's wrong? Talk to me," he commanded, striding across the room to where Ellie was standing.

"You'll think I'm crazy," Ellie replied, leaning into Scott's body as he wrapped his arms around her. He was reassuringly bulky, easily dwarfing her own petite frame.

"I very much doubt that."

Ellie shrugged. "It was just a bad dream." She hoped that Scott wouldn't press for details, assuming that if he did, he'd dismiss anything she said as nothing more than a product of her imagination.

"Hmmm." Ellie felt Scott's reply as it rumbled throughout her entire body.

"Honestly, I'm fine. I just got lost in my own thoughts for a while there." Ellie pulled away from Scott and smiled. "It's a big day today, we've got a lot to do, if you're still okay to help, that is?"

"Of course I am. Are you worried that you're extorting labour from me? Is that it? Because you are. You know that, right?"

"I am not!" Ellie exclaimed, smacking Scott lightly on the arm.

Scott pulled Ellie back into him and kissed her gently. "Even if you were, I'd do anything for you," he said softly. "I've been in love with you since I was a teenager. These last few weeks have been… well, they've been amazing."

Ellie smiled brightly. It never got old hearing Scott proclaim his undying devotion for her. "Maybe you should show me how much I mean to you," she suggested, sliding her arms around his neck, pulling him down to her so that she could kiss him much more forcefully than he'd kissed her.

"I thought you said we had a long day ahead of us," Scott replied when he got the chance.

"We do." Ellie frowned faintly. She had a long list of things that she wanted to get done. The whole apartment needed a coat of paint, a new television unit that she'd bought needed to be built, and then she had to unpack. "But Emma and Blake are not due until ten," she finished, smiling coyly.

Chapter 2 – Emma
Monday 27th May 2019

"Ellie!" I shouted, hammering on her front door. Blake had most of what we'd brought with us, but my own arms were starting to complain at how much I'd had to carry up three flights of stairs, there being only so much I could palm off on Blake.

"Why are we doing this again?" Blake asked.

"It's the right thing to do," I explained for the umpteenth time through gritted teeth. Blake was not really sold on the idea of a painting party. Helping Ellie transform Joanne's old apartment into her new home was not that high up on his list of priorities.

"We should be trying to translate the prophecy," Blake muttered, referring to the scroll that had been passed down through the generations of Ellie's family. We'd only learned of its existence recently because Joanne had kept it hidden from Ellie. Joanne had kept a lot of things hidden from Ellie, including the fact that she believed my life needed to be sacrificed for the sake of the world.

I rolled my eyes before answering, "We've been through this already."

"There must be a way." Blake was quite adamant on this point. I knew because we'd had this argument several times already.

"Go on then, explain it to me. Exactly how are we going to translate something that's written in an old angelic script?"

"There must be a way," Blake repeated, frowning.

"Maybe there is, maybe there isn't, but at the minute, I'm still stuck on the fact that even you can't read it." Blake knew every language that had ever been spoken in his lifetime. That was one of the perks of his job. When he reaped (or cleaved) a soul, he bore witness to the person's life, so there was nothing he didn't know. Well, that wasn't quite true, there was a lot he didn't know, but he was good at human history. He just didn't know all that much about the supernatural world; we were learning about that together.

"Abaddon will—"

"Abaddon won't do anything," I cut Blake off. "We've heard nothing from her in weeks, not a peep. We're on our own here."

"She can't be the only angel on Earth."

"No, she can't, but you've never seen another one, and even with Ellie's new ability to *see*, she's not seen one either."

"She hasn't looked."

"She's had enough on her plate," I said, turning to look at Blake. "We've all had enough on our plates. Look, I know you're worried about what might happen in the future but can't we just try and have some fun today? Don't we deserve a day off?" Blake had been overly cautious ever since we'd battled a vindictive ghost, although he would deny it. He'd also correct my language, saying that a ghost was a Hollywood invention and that the correct term was 'remnant.'

Blake glanced in my direction so that he could look me in the eye, and I was suddenly ambushed by his thoughts and emotions. He was afraid, but not just afraid, he was terrified.

"Oh, Blake." I sighed, overcome with guilt for not realising how deep his fear ran. "Why haven't you talked to me about what's going on in that head of yours?"

"I don't want to talk about it."

"You need to talk about it. It will help," I promised, mentally kicking myself in the shins. In many ways, Blake was like a child, despite his age. He'd spent most of his existence as a spectre, cut off from his fellow man because he only existed on this plane when he was with me. He wasn't very well equipped to deal with emotional distress. And I should have known he was suffering; I could literally sense his emotions, and sometimes I could read his mind. That was one of the advantages of dating him as opposed to dating a regular Joe. Mind you, I wasn't sure if 'advantage' was the right word because it worked both ways, and he was much better at reading my mind than I was his. When he was around, my thoughts were never really my own. Somehow, though, I didn't think that was a fair justification for having missed what was going on with him.

"Talk to—" I started to say before the door swung open. "Ellie!" I plastered a smile on my face and then saw that it was my brother behind the door, not Ellie. "Oh, it's you," I finished, somewhat less brightly.

"Top of the morning to you too, my lovely little sister," Scott replied, beaming from ear to ear. "Come in. Ellie's just in the shower."

Ellie's new apartment wasn't all that big. The front door opened straight into the living area. To the left, there was an open-plan kitchen-diner, and to the right, there was a bedroom and the bathroom. And over there, in that corner, that one right there, that was where Joanne had tried to kill me. Perhaps Blake wasn't the only one who was carrying around some emotional baggage. Perhaps that was how I'd missed his suffering; I was too busy wallowing in my own. Ellie had assured me that today would be therapeutic. We were going to 'wash away the bad memories with some brightly-coloured paint and some new furniture.' That was what she'd said anyway.

"Come in, come in," Scott broke into my thoughts. I'd stopped just inside the doorway. "You're letting all the cold air in."

"What cold air?" I argued. "There's a carpeted hallway outside of Ellie's front door. Besides which, it's a nice day."

"It's just a saying." Scott smirked at me. "Now get your backside in here, won't you?" He pulled me further into the room and gave me a quick hug. "Blake," he added when he released hold of me.

"Scott." Blake nodded. If Scott thought that he could intimidate Blake with one-word statements, then he was sadly mistaken. He had no idea who he was dealing with.

"Why don't I put the kettle on?" I suggested, disrupting the tension that was mounting between the two men while muttering to myself, *Give me strength.*

I heard that.

I thought you liked Scott. I might not have been talking to Blake but seeing as he'd replied…

I don't think he likes me.

He doesn't know you. Scott hadn't spent all that much time with Blake yet, primarily because Blake didn't like spending time with anyone other than me. *He's just sizing you up because you're dating his little sister. He might act like a bit of a tool sometimes, but he's protective of me. He takes after Dad.*

If you say so.

"Nice place, isn't it?" I remarked out loud, effectively ending my conversation with Blake. The kettle was forgotten because the sofa kept drawing my eye. Cautiously I took a step towards it. I'd been sitting there when Joanne had tried to poison me. If not for Blake, she'd probably have succeeded. I kind of got it; she'd been brought up to believe that if ever I met Blake, I'd be forced to make him open a portal into Hell because I was the Key. Demons would flood the Earth and life as we knew it would be over. I kind of got it, but I clearly wasn't over it. I dumped everything that I was carrying onto the sofa, forcing myself to acknowledge what had happened. And that was only a small part of what I'd had to deal with recently!

"Yeah, it's great. I still can't believe that Joanne's had this place ever since Grandpa Harold died." Scott was clearly oblivious to what was going on in my head.

"I know, crazy huh?" I answered when Scott cleared his throat, interrupting my thoughts. "Why did she buy it again?" I asked, knowing full well why she'd bought it. She'd bought it because she'd needed somewhere to stash the prophecy and the angel blade that had come with it, but I didn't think that was the official story, and Scott lived in blissful ignorance still. I wanted to tell him all about Blake, my lineage, and Ellie's heritage, but Ellie wanted to keep him in the dark, believing he'd be safer that way.

"Apparently, she thought it would make a better investment than stocks or shares. Personally, I think she was mistaken, but it's worked out all right for Ellie. Joanne signed it over to her last week; she now owns it outright."

"Yeah, she said," I answered, still focussed on the sofa.

"What exactly is it that you're looking at?" Scott asked, taking a step towards me. "I know it's a nice view, but it's not that nice," he concluded, assuming I was looking out of the window.

"Nothing, honestly, I'm fine." I shrugged and made myself turn towards Scott, a smile on my face.

"Uh-huh, if you say so. You and Ellie are both acting a little odd this morning."

"Why? What's wrong with Ellie?" I was immediately concerned.

"She had a nightmare. She doesn't want to talk about it though. Well, she won't talk to me about it anyway. Maybe she'll open up to you."

"Maybe... I'll ask her about it later," I replied, staring hard at my brother. He'd sounded so vulnerable and unsure, which was not like him. If anything, I'd have said he was usually overconfident. "So," I changed the subject, I had enough of my own problems to deal with, "has Ellie told you what she's got planned for us today?"

"All I know is that it involves manual labour and paint," Scott answered.

"Let me guess, by the end of the day, the whole place will be yellow."

"Hey!" Ellie exclaimed, putting in an appearance at last and interrupting my back and forth with Scott. "I'm not that obvious, am I? Blake, come on in," she finished, beaming at him. Blake had remained standing by the door while Scott and I had been talking. He wasn't all that great in social situations, but with Ellie's encouragement, he eventually took a step towards the kitchen and deposited the box he was carrying on the kitchen counter.

"Go on then," I answered, giving Ellie a quick hug, "tell me what colour we're painting your bedroom."

"Erm… it's a new shade that I found online. It's called Lemon Spiral," Ellie said with a grin.

"I see," I raised my eyebrows. "And the lounge?"

"Ah well, I didn't want the whole place to be the same colour, so I've out picked something a little different for in here. It's called Homey Honey."

"Which is what colour exactly?"

"Weeell… it's sort of a creamy-yellowy colour." Ellie managed to keep a straight face for a few seconds before she burst out laughing.

"Uh-huh." I nodded, a smile lifting the corners of my own mouth. "And that's why Blake and I bought you these." I retrieved a bouquet of flowers from where I'd dumped them on the sofa.

"Oh! They're beautiful!" And in my humble opinion, they were. Knowing Ellie as I did, I'd chosen a brightly coloured spray that mixed white antirrhinums with a vivid yellow freesia, some pale-yellow roses, and a few sprigs of green foliage. "But I don't have a vase." Ellie wrinkled her nose in dismay.

"On it," I reassured. "Blake?"

Blake didn't answer, but he did lift the vase that we'd brought with us out of the box that he'd carried.

"Amazing! You're the best." Ellie smiled at me but went to hug Blake. I felt a ripple of shock send shivers down my spine when Ellie wrapped her arms around him. Blake had never been touched by anyone other than me.

Hug her back, I said to Blake, taking advantage of our ability to talk mind-to-mind.

Ellie, who couldn't possibly have known about the reassurance I'd given Blake, hung on in there until he did as I'd suggested and squeezed her gently. Perhaps she'd just decided that today was the day we were removing the grim from the Grim Reaper! "We're going to have such a fun day," she declared, letting go of Blake and taking the vase from him before busying herself in the kitchen with the flowers. It sounded like she was trying to convince herself rather than me, though, and that had me slightly worried. Ellie was usually the life and soul of the party. If she needed convincing that it was going to be a good day, then I wasn't so sure that it was going to turn out that way.

It was surprising how quickly Ellie put us to work after that. In no time at all, Blake and Scott were deployed in the bedroom while Ellie and I were left to paint the lounge. Thankfully there wasn't a great deal of furniture to move. All we had to work around was the sofa, a bookcase, and Ellie's boxes.

"I thought you'd have wanted to work alongside Scott," I commented after we'd spread out some dust sheets and popped the top off a can of paint.

"You mean, you wanted to work alongside Blake," Ellie replied.

"Well, yes… always. But it's not just that. I'm worried about the two of them getting on. They don't really know each other, and Blake is well… Blake."

"And that's exactly why I put them to work together. We need our menfolk to be comfortable in each other's company. We spend a lot of time with each other after all."

"That's true." I nodded in agreement before pausing to admire the section of wall that I'd been rollering. The colour was nice, it wasn't such a harsh yellow that the place would look sickly when it was done, and it wasn't so bright that it would look too intense. Instead, it looked comfortable and inviting. Somehow the paint manufacturer had captured the essence of a warm sunny day. "So, do you want to tell me about your nightmare?" I asked, going back to my rollering.

"Scott told you about that, did he?"

"He might have mentioned it. He's worried about you."

"It was just a dream."

"Tell me about it anyway."

"Urgh, it was… awful, Emma, just awful." Ellie shuddered before describing in detail what she'd dreamt about. When she explained how I'd been forced to call Blake to me, I couldn't help but wince at the thought of what she'd—we'd—suffered. "Anyway, it was just a dream. What else could it have been?" she eventually concluded.

I rolled my eyes before answering, "Didn't I say the same thing when I first met Blake?"

Ellie turned to look at me, her face grave. "That was a little different, wouldn't you say?"

"Was it? Maybe when Abaddon gave you the ability to *see,* she also gave you the power of premonition. She wasn't exactly explicit about what you'd be able to do with her gifts." I emphasised the word 'gifts' with air quotes between one roller stroke and the next.

"Well, no, she wasn't. But surely she'd have said if I could see the future."

"Maybe, maybe not. We don't know all that much about her, do we? All we know for sure is that she's an angel and that she created the line of guardians because God told her to. And," I continued, a new thought occurring, "if we're being really honest about it," I tilted my head in Ellie's direction, "we don't even know that for a fact. We only have her word on the matter."

"I don't think she'd lie. Why would she?" That was Ellie, always looking for the best in people while I was suspicious about everyone and everything. "And if we do believe what she said, we also know that she injected her blood into my great-grandmother's womb to create the line of guardians. That's how come I have angel blood in my veins. Oh, and we also know that the blood has to be activated with an angel's kiss."

"True… I wonder if any angel will do, or if it has to be Abaddon's kiss."

"Who knows." Ellie sighed. "I keep hoping that she'll turn up so I can ask a few more questions. She was quite adamant that I should kill you though. Maybe she's staying away because I said I wouldn't."

"Maybe, but there *has* to be another way." I sounded adamant, but I was starting to wonder myself. What if my confidence was misplaced? "Whatever happens, I won't let your dream come true. I'd rather kill myself before letting anyone use me to get to Blake. It's not like I want Hell on Earth either."

"Emma!" Ellie gasped.

I didn't think that my comment was that extreme. "What?" I was genuinely confused by Ellie's reaction. At the end of the day, I kind of, sort of agreed with Joanne that no one person's life was more important than the fate of mankind. I just didn't like that it was my life we were talking about.

"You're bleeding," Ellie exclaimed, abandoning her roller in the paint tray before dashing into the kitchen for some tissue.

"I am? Where from?" I asked, arbitrarily looking around before inspecting each of my hands.

"Emma, get over here!" Ellie shouted at me, forcing me to dump my own roller and follow her. "Your nose," she explained, offering me some kitchen roll. "How many is that now?"

"Bugger!" I wiped my face with the back of my hand, smearing blood from my nose and paint from my hands across my cheek. "That's five now, two in the last week." Nosebleeds were becoming part and parcel of being soulmates with the Grim Reaper, not that we were soulmates in the truest sense of the word. We actually shared a soul between us, and one of the things that Abaddon had explained to Ellie was that the more I used my half of the soul, the more unwell I'd become.

I took a step closer to Ellie, felt a strange popping sensation, and heard Scott swear loudly in the bedroom over my shoulder. Ellie and I looked at each other for only a brief moment before realising what had happened. Blake was only corporeal when he was by my side. Clearly I'd stepped too far away from him. Quickly, I turned on heel and headed in the direction of where Blake and Scott were. I felt it the second that Blake was safely back inside of my bubble. The strange sensation of him materialising once again.

"Shit!" I muttered quietly.

"Holy mother of... what the f—"

Cutting Scott off, I asked, "Everything all right in here?"

Peering into the bedroom from the doorway, I could see Blake standing on one side of the room scowling, a paintbrush at his feet, with Scott on the other, his jaw on the floor. Not literally, of course.

"Blake just bloody well disappeared." Scott's eyes were wide open. He'd have looked a little comical if the situation wasn't so serious.

"Pfft, don't be silly, Scott. People don't just disappear," I pooh-poohed, wrinkling up my nose.

"He did, and I can prove it. He was covered in paint a minute ago. It's like he's never done any bloody decorating before today. Look at him now; he's perfectly clean."

I glanced at Blake, who shrugged ever so slightly. Scott was right. Blake didn't have a mark on him, but at least he'd reappeared in the same outfit that he'd started the day in. Blake's appearance was nothing more than a physical manifestation of what he believed himself to look like. Unconstrained by my bubble (as we'd termed my sphere of influence), he could literally take on any appearance that he wanted. Today, I'd suggested he appear wearing jeans and a rugby top. "Scott, come on," I reasoned. "People don't just vanish. Maybe the paint fumes are getting to you."

"The paint fumes are not getting to me, Emma. Something strange is going on. Now tell me what the hell it is, or I'll... I'll—"

"You'll what? Tell Dad on me?"

"I might," Scott declared hotly. His face had turned a bright scarlet colour. "Come on, fess up. What are you hiding?" Scott's question hung in the air unanswered for what felt like an eternity. "Well?" he demanded.

The fight drained from my body. I glanced over my shoulder at Ellie and raised an eyebrow. "I think we should just tell him," I said.

"I don't suppose we've really got a choice now, have we?" she replied, a strange catch in her voice.

"Blake?" I asked, wanting him to agree with my decision.

You didn't ask my opinion when you wanted to tell Ellie about me. He chose to answer silently.

I know, and I'm sorry. I should have done, but this was all new to me then. I needed to tell someone. I needed to tell Ellie.

Fine.

Fine as in you're okay with me telling Scott?

Yes.

"What's going on?" Scott interrupted.

"I was just talking to Blake," I answered.

"No, you weren't, you didn't say a word."

"I did, you just couldn't hear me."

"Before we start," Ellie interrupted, "can we carry on painting while we talk? I'd like my apartment done by the end of the day. Pleeeaaassseee, there's a takeaway in it for you all if we're done by teatime," she bartered, breaking the growing tension that had thickened the air like glue.

Scott smiled briefly at Ellie before scowling at me. "As it is, we're pretty much done in here, so let's regroup in the lounge when we've tidied up, and then you'd better start talking, Emma."

"Hey! Why do you assume I'm the one with a story to tell?"

Before Scott could answer, Ellie jumped to my defence. "Actually, Scott, we all need to tell you something."

Chapter 3 – Emma
Monday 27th May 2019

The longer we'd talked, the more wound-up Scott had gotten. At first, he'd thought it was all a big joke, then he'd accused me of all sorts—being crazy, lying.... In the end, he'd stormed out, leaving Ellie in tears and me a little shell-shocked. Only Blake seemed unconcerned.

"He's such a dick," I muttered, shaking my head.

"Don't say that," Ellie replied a little morosely. She was sitting cross-legged on the floor, on one of the dust sheets that we'd spread out earlier on. She had a paintbrush in one hand and was idly flicking its bristles with the other. She hadn't done any painting in a while.

"Well, he is," I snapped. "You didn't behave like a little child when I told you about Blake."

"No, I didn't, but you'd been talking to me about Blake for a while before you announced that he was the Grim Reaper."

Blake's displeasure rippled across my skin, but I ignored it. "Announced?"

Ellie glanced in my direction. "You know what I mean."

I clenched my teeth together before replying. I wasn't really annoyed with Ellie after all. "What are we going to do?"

"Maybe I should try and find him."

"Actually, I should probably try and find him. It's me that he's angry with."

"I've never seen him like that before now." Fresh tears leaked from the corners of Ellie's eyes.

"Well, I guess no one's ever told him that angels and demons are real," I replied, trying to give Scott the benefit of the doubt.

"He hates me."

"What? No, he doesn't!" I exclaimed, dropping onto the floor beside Ellie and wrapping my arms around her, ignoring the still wet paintbrush in her hands.

"He does." Ellie cried harder. "He thinks I sided with you when I should have sided with him."

"Oh, Ellie, he doesn't think that at all; he's just confused. We did drop quite the bombshell on him." I did my best to soothe Ellie while also speaking to Blake. *Blake, would you go and find Scott, please.* I looked over the top of Ellie's head at Blake. He'd finished the last of the painting and appeared to be admiring his handiwork.

I don't know where he is. Blake continued to stare at the wall.

I don't either. Maybe he's gone home. Or maybe he's gone for a walk. Can you just go and have a look? Please?

Blake turned to face me. *You're worried about him?*

Of course I'm worried about him. He's my brother.

I thought you were angry with him.

Well… I'm that too.

Blake stared at me for a while. Random images flicked in my mind's eye, and I realised that he was trying to understand another of life's many mysteries. I was furious with my brother because he hadn't immediately believed me, but I was also worried about him. I was bothered that he might do something rash. I loved him, of course I did, he was my brother, but right now, I was really pissed at him, while also trying not to be for Ellie's sake. In the end, all Blake said was 'fine,' and then he stepped through the wall and out of the apartment.

"There!" I declared. "Blake's gone to find Scott. He'll bring him back, and we'll sort everything out."

Ellie didn't even have time to reply before Blake reappeared.

"That was quick," I said out loud so as to include Ellie in the conversation.

"He's in the hall, at the end of the corridor."

Ellie jerked herself free of my embrace. "Why didn't you bring him back?"

"He's outside of Emma's bubble," Blake replied.

I put my arm out in front of Ellie's chest before she had time to move. "It's okay. I'll go and get him."

"But—"

"No buts, Ellie. It's me he's angry with." I repeated what I'd said earlier. "I'll go and talk to him."

"He's angry with me too."

"Don't be silly. He loves you." I patted Ellie's hand before hauling myself up from off the floor.

Blake was right; Scott hadn't made it far at all. Ellie's apartment was the end one on her floor. Scott had only gotten as far as the lifts in the centre of the building.

"Scott!" I called. It wasn't the most inspired of greetings, but I had to start somewhere.

"I thought I made it perfectly clear that I wanted to be on my own," Scott barked at me.

"No, actually, you didn't." My own temper was still simmering away quite nicely, even if I'd suggested otherwise to Ellie. "You accused me of being crazy. You accused me of lying. I think you even managed to imply that Blake has somehow brainwashed me, but you never said that you wanted to be on your own."

"Well, I do, so buzz off."

"I'm not going anywhere." I folded my arms across my chest. "Not until you come up with a reasonable explanation for leaving Ellie in tears." I knew exactly where to strike.

Scott stilled. "Ellie's in tears?"

"Of course she's in tears, you jackass. You basically called her a liar."

"I did not. I called you a liar."

I let my arms fall. "But Ellie believes me because she knows that I'm telling the truth."

Scott's shoulders sagged. "You can't be telling the truth. You just can't."

"Why not? Because you don't like it? Because you have another explanation for how Blake vanished into thin air?"

"But… I just…" Scott's voice trailed off into nothing. He ran a hand through his hair, giving me an idea; perhaps the unexplainable was how to prove to Scott that there was more to life than we'd always believed.

Blake, I called. *Would you come here for a minute? Please? I know I'm asking a lot today.*

Surprisingly, Blake complied. He was still confused by my warring emotions, and I think he wanted to see for himself what Scott and I were talking about.

"Holy sh—"

"Now, now, Scott," I interrupted, having expected his reaction, or at least one like it. "There's no need for that kind of language, thank you very much."

"But… how is this possible?"

"Never mind that." I smacked him across the chest. "What are you going to say to Ellie?"

"Ellie!" Scott's eyes clouded with worry at the mention of her name, and then he took off towards her apartment.

Blake took a step in the same direction, but I stayed put. "Let's give them a minute." I caught hold of Blake's arm and pulled him back to me. "Thank you," I whispered, sliding my arms around his neck and pressing my body into his.

"For what?" Blake asked.

I shrugged before answering. "For everything." And then I touched my lips to his. I knew that Blake was puzzled, I could feel it swirling around in my gut, but that didn't stop him from turning my gentle kiss into something much more heated. He pushed me up against the lift door while his tongue sought out mine. It was a while before we made it back to Ellie's apartment, and then Scott wanted a replay of everything we'd already told him.

Of course, there were some things that Scott hadn't needed to be appraised of. He'd known that I'd been stalked and attacked some months back. That was common knowledge because there was nothing supernatural about being stalked by a nutter. What he hadn't known was that Seith, Blake's guardian, a spectral dog-like beast, had ended my attacker's life, saving mine in the process. Scott, like everyone else, had believed that a rabid dog had intervened that day and I'd just been lucky.

Scott had also known that I'd ended up in hospital a few weeks ago because of a 'gas explosion,' but he hadn't known that the gas explosion was nothing of the sort. In reality, a ghost had taken against me. Juiced up on a dark soul that Blake had missed (okay, he'd failed to cleave it because of me, but that's a long story!), the ghost had bound me in place with scalding hot water from a tap. The explosion had actually been Blake. He'd taken umbrage and attacked the bathroom with his scythe.

"How the f—" Scott started to say, our jobs long since forgotten.

"Scott!" I interjected.

"How is it that you two," he started again, rolling his eyes before indicating me and Ellie with a nod of his head, "have not needed to be admitted to an asylum after everything that's happened?"

"I don't know. Maybe we're just more accepting than you are?"

"You lying ratbag!" Ellie laughed. Scott's apology had obviously been a good one because by the time Blake and I had made it back to Ellie's apartment, she'd been all smiles again. "You spent months barely able to leave your house."

"I left my house."

"Only when you had to. After you were attacked, you hid yourself away."

"I did not."

"You did too. It took arguing with Jennifer at the hospital to snap you out of the funk you'd gotten yourself into."

"Well... even if that's true," I conceded, "I didn't freak out when I found out who Blake was or that we were soulmates."

"No, you accepted that quite well actually," Ellie said before laughing out loud. "Do you remember when you introduced me to Blake? You made him go to the bottom of your garden, and when he stepped outside of your bubble, I nearly wet myself. I desperately tried to come up with another explanation for what I'd seen. Any other explanation would have done."

Ellie's laughter was infectious, and I couldn't help but laugh along with her. Blake had been sampling some jam straight from the jar at the time, and when he'd turned incorporeal, it had simply dropped to the ground, much like his paintbrush today. "Poor Blake," I shook my head, "we peppered you with a hundred different questions that day, didn't we?" I reached over to rest my hand gently on his knee by way of an apology.

"You did," Blake agreed. He'd remained silent while Ellie and I had recanted everything that had gone on, but I'd felt a brief spike of pure, unadulterated bliss when I'd mentioned our first kiss.

We all fell silent for a few minutes before Ellie spoke up again. "It's odd, isn't it?" She frowned. "Both of us accepted Blake and Abaddon for what they are without any real qualms."

For what we are? Blake demanded silently, his anger erupting from nothing within a millisecond. *I'm not an animal.*

Poor choice of words on Ellie's behalf, I apologised.

We should go, Blake snapped.

We've not eaten yet. I'd long ago clocked that the way to Blake's heart was through his stomach. I didn't get a reply, but Blake's temper did cool by a couple of degrees.

Ellie carried on speaking, not realising that Blake and I had had a heated exchange. "It's been the actions of real live people that have caused us the most bother. Peter Collins, my mum…" Her voice trailed off into nothing. "I wonder why that is."

"I can't believe I'm about to say this, but maybe it's because Emma has half of Blake's soul and you have angel blood in your veins?" Scott answered. He'd clearly been paying attention, although I wasn't convinced that he believed what we'd told him yet. "Maybe you're both predisposed to accept the unnatural."

Unnatural! Blake exploded, and I'd been so close to calming him down.

"Guys, can we change the subject?" I asked, earning myself a hard stare from Ellie and a confused glance from Scott. "Maybe we could order some dinner?" I suggested.

"Now that does sound like a good idea." Scott laid aside his confusion in an instant. "What do you fancy? Pizza?"

"Blake's never had pizza before," I answered. He was still fuming, but I felt his intrigue dance across my skin.

"You've never had pizza?" Scott asked, shaking his head in disbelief. "Crikey, you really haven't lived, have you? How did you cope?"

"What choice did I have?"

Scott huffed. "I really feel for you, man. A life without pizza isn't worth living. What shall we have, a twelve-inch meat feast and some garlic bread? Go big or go home, right?"

"Er, no! I want ham and mushroom," Ellie said.

"And I want barbecue chicken and pineapple," I added.

"No one puts pineapple on a pizza; that's just wrong." Scott dismissed my ideal set of toppings.

"Well, I like it," I declared hotly.

"Calm down, children," Ellie waded into the argument before it could really get going. I could almost hear her wondering if this was what the rest of her life was going to be like now that she was dating my brother. Yes, Ellie, yes, it was! "This is my treat, seeing as how you all helped me out today, so order whatever you like. Everyone can have their own pizza, and Blake, have what *you* want, and feel free to try everyone else's."

Somehow Ellie had managed to soothe Blake's temper, and he turned his attention to choosing a pizza. In the end, he settled on a fairly basic four cheese delight, despite Scott doing his best to persuade him to try out a new chicken curry offering. His anticipation mounted with every second that passed until the buzzer sounded to indicate that the delivery man had arrived, and then he hovered over Ellie while she paid.

"Does anyone want a plate?" Ellie asked, taking receipt of four nine-inch pizzas, two garlic breads, and a bottle of pop.

"No, let's just eat out of the boxes to save on the washing up," I replied. "And please, will you give Blake his already? He looks like he's got ants in his pants!" I remarked out loud before adding silently, *It might be hot, Blake.*

Blake didn't reply. He didn't quite snatch his pizza from Ellie, but common courtesy was most definitely out of the window, and he didn't bother to sit down before diving in.

Mmm, this is good. Why haven't we had pizza before now? he asked me.

It's not really my favourite food, I answered. Pizza just didn't do it for me. That said, I did perch myself on the edge of the sofa and start in on mine. It might not have been my favourite food, but I was hungry. It had ended up being an exhausting day. I wanted to nestle in among cushions and really let myself relax, but I found that I couldn't. Even with the room's make-over (that still needed to be finished off), the sofa still sparked little waves of anxiety in my gut.

Blake, feeling my distress, glanced in my direction. *I'm fine,* I reassured. *It's in the past. I just need to get over it.*

Maybe Ellie should have moved somewhere else.

Maybe, but it's difficult to say no when you're offered somewhere like this for free.

She could have sold it.

That would have taken time. She needed somewhere to live now. It's okay, I promise.

Blake raised an eyebrow but didn't comment further, happy to eat his pizza. Contentment wrapped itself around me.

I'd barely touched my dinner when a sharp, stinging sensation in my head brought tears to my eyes. I reached up to wipe my cheeks, but as my hand made contact with my face, the pain exploded.

"Argh," I cried out, dropping my pizza so that I could press my hands to my temples. Blake was by my side in an instant, his own pizza presumably discarded somewhere.

"Emma, what is it? What's wrong?" Ellie asked, her voice distant and indistinct. I could barely make out the words.

"My head," I sobbed. The pain was beyond anything I'd ever felt before. If someone had stabbed me through the eye with a screwdriver, I don't think it could have been any worse. "It hurts," I cried, my vision wavering.

"I'll ring for an ambulance," I heard Scott say, but he was a million miles away from where I was.

"No, don't. There's nothing they can do," I said. Or at least, I think that's what I said. My words came out slurred as the darkness overtook me and I passed happily into oblivion.

It took a long time for me to realise that I'd woken up. An all-encompassing black cloud had wrapped me in a comforting embrace. I couldn't see anything, not even my own hand when I waved it in front of my face. I'd gone blind, that was the only possible explanation.

"Hello?" I called. "Blake? Ellie?" I assumed my friends had seen me stir, but no one answered. *Maybe they've put me in Ellie's bed.* I reached out to touch my surroundings. Ellie's duvet was a plush one, and her cover was white with yellow embroidery tracing a circular pattern across it. My hand should have sunk into the soft brushed cotton; I should have been able to feel the stitching as if it had been etched into the material. Instead, I felt nothing. Literally nothing. I was suspended in space, held in thin air by an unseen force. A growing sense of alarm clawed at me, threatening to overwhelm me, tempting me to give in to hysteria.

"H… hello?" I said again. "Is… erm… is anyone there?"

"Ah, you're awake at last," a female voice replied.

"Who… who's that? Who… who are you?" I stuttered. Fear held onto my words, keeping them trapped in my mouth, making it hard for me to speak.

"Don't be afraid. You're safe, and you know me."

"I… I do?" I asked, thinking about what I did know, what I'd been able to ascertain. Whoever had spoken to me was evidently a woman and she had a slight accent, but other than that… nothing. I had nothing!

"You do."

"Who are you then? And where are we?" I asked. My lungs still felt like they were being crushed by a vice, and my heart continued to beat frenetically in my chest, but the swelling in my throat had abated slightly.

"We're in your head, child. And you know me, we've met before."

We're in my head? That was new. "Have we? I… I can't see you."

"Maybe a little light will help," the woman replied, snapping her fingers so close to my face that I felt a cold blast of air tickle my nose.

All of a sudden, a bright light flared in front of my eyes, forcing me to look away. I was blind again, but this time the more I blinked, the more my surroundings came into focus, not that there were any surroundings for me to focus on. I was in some sort of void, like the one that Ellie had dreamed of. Although at least when Ellie had dreamed of such a place, she'd had the foresight to make it white in colour.

"We're in your head, dear. You can make it look however you want," the woman said, even though I hadn't voiced my thoughts aloud. And as my eyes adjusted to the light, I could at last see who was speaking. She could have been my twin. She had the same colour hair as me, the same colour eyes, even the shape of her nose was the same.

"You're me," I exclaimed, panic finally giving way to bewilderment.

"Not quite. Try again."

I stared harder and realised that although the woman facing me did look like me, she looked older. Finally, the truth dawned on me. "You're one of my ancestors."

"Not *just* one of the ancestors," she corrected with a head toss. "I'm *the* ancestor, the first of your line." She seemed so regal sitting opposite from me. I felt like a small infant in the presence of a god. "Oh no, child. I'm nothing of the sort," she laughed, answering my unspoken comment again.

"How are you doing that?" I asked.

"I keep telling you: we're in your head."

That didn't even begin to make sense, but I nodded anyway. "What's your name?" I asked, changing the subject, my breathing finally returning to normal.

"Johnna," she replied. I didn't comment, but clearly the look of confusion on my face was enough because she carried on without prompting, "Mother named me after him."

"Johnna," I tried to pronounce the woman's name correctly, "sounds nothing like Blake."

"Don't be silly." Johnna tutted. "She named me after John, not Blake. She always said that he was my father, that he died before I was born."

I wrinkled my nose while I thought it through before conceding, "Well, that was kind of true I guess."

"Hmmm," she hummed in response. "It was only after I died that I learned the truth. We've only ever learned the truth after our deaths. Until you, that is. You found him."

"And now I'm dying, aren't I?"

"Not quite yet, dear. You're unconscious, that's true, but there's a bit of life left in you still. Blake would have known if you were dying, and he'd have told you, wouldn't he?"

Some of the tension eased in my shoulders. "That's true. How long have I got left?"

"That depends."

"On what?"

"On many things. If Abaddon had had her way, you'd be dead already. But she's starting to realise that killing you won't solve her problems. And Blake would never use the scythe on you, so she knows that she can't count on a cleaving. No, now that Blake knows of your existence and that souls are passed down through the generations, he'll simply wait for the next in line to be born. With the way things are going, that'll most likely be Ellie's child."

"But won't my soul be passed on to my children?"

"And if you don't have children?"

"Well… then I guess it would go to Sc… Oh! I see." I blushed thinking about Ellie and Scott, and the more I tried not to think about them together, the more stubbornly the idea remained rooted in my mind.

Johnna raised an eyebrow before continuing. "Abaddon doesn't want her bloodline mixing with yours, but she really doesn't want one of her guardians having your soul for their own, so she'll help to keep you alive for a while yet, and she'll help you find another way to stop the portal from being opened."

"There's another way?"

"There's always another way," Johnna answered confidently.

"How?"

"You need to call on the power of your ancestors when the time is right. You'll see in due course."

"If you say so," I muttered, not fully understanding. "How is it that you're here?" I asked. "Able to communicate with me?" I clarified. "I assume no one else has their ancestors in their head."

Johnna chuckled. "No, you're special… unique. In fact, we're special." She paused, tilting her head to one side, gathering her thoughts perhaps. "As most people grow and age, their spirit, the essence of who they are, becomes infused with some of the energy of creation from their soul. It, the spirit, becomes an entity in its own right."

"Uh-huh," I nodded along as Johnna spoke, sort of getting what she was saying.

"Our spirits do not."

"We don't have spirits?" I interrupted, alarmed.

"We do, of course we do. But our spirits remain fused with our soul. Most souls grow and swell, you see. The energy is always fluid, so it's able to seep into the spirit. The golden soul—the one that you share with Blake—it's not like that. It's powerful, but it's unchanging. There was only ever meant to be one Keeper of Souls, you see."

"Sooo…?" I prompted.

"So, my spirit, and the spirits of all of your ancestors are a part of you. They're a part of your soul."

"Oookaaay," I replied, pulling a face. "That kind of makes sense. Why didn't you speak to me when I was a child though? I thought I was hallucinating the first time I saw you in the mirror."

"We've never spoken to the living until you. We made a decision to let each child live out their own life without interference from us."

"But then I met Blake?"

Johnna nodded in agreement. "But then you met Blake, and we've done what we could to help you."

"This is amaz—" I started to say, but a strange tugging sensation in the pit of my stomach made me pause. Something, or someone, was clawing at my innards. I wrapped my arms around my body and groaned. "What's happening?"

Johnna smiled. "It's okay. You're waking up, that's all."

"But I still have questions."

"And we'll still be here. We'll always be here. And Emma, remember what I told you. There's always another way, use the power of your ancestors when the ti…" Her voice faded, and a feeling of electricity jolted me upright.

Chapter 4 – Blake
Monday 27th May 2019 / Tuesday 28th May 2019

Blake stood watching Emma sleep, his thoughts racing. Her breathing was deep and even, but he found himself unable to relax. She seemed quite content despite blacking out earlier on in the day. In fact, she'd been somewhat animated when she'd come round, excited even, chatting away quite happily about her vision, Johnna (who she was and what she'd said), and what she'd learned, but he'd been left on edge by what had happened. In the end, after both Emma and Ellie had started to yawn, he'd persuaded Emma that it was time for them to leave. He was still tense now and his shoulder throbbed uncomfortably. He knew that Emma would say his shoulder couldn't possibly be bothering him, that not only was it fully healed, but it was like it'd never been injured at all. Logically, he knew that she was right, but that didn't stop the dull, persistent ache from irritating him. Absently, he reached up and rubbed the exact spot where a tree root had pierced his flesh weeks previously, introducing him to a world of pain.

Blake had never felt anything before he'd met Emma. Only with her could he experience the world around him: the tickle of his hair as it blew across his face, the coarse texture of his shirt on his shoulders, the tired ache of his feet after standing for too long. These were all new sensations for him. He'd been woefully unprepared for the agony of having skin and muscle torn apart.

When the tree root, controlled by Anais Bechard, a remnant who'd managed to retain her soul, had been wrenched from the ground, spraying mud in every direction, Blake had arrogantly dismissed the threat as nothing of the sort. After all, he'd watched from the sidelines as the Black Death had swept across the world killing millions, spreading from Asia through the Mediterranean Basin before striking into the heart of Africa and the rest of Europe. He'd witnessed both the American and the French Revolutions, in some cases walking through gunfire with a distinct lack of concern for his well-being, safe in the knowledge that any stray bullets would pass harmlessly through him. But as his blood had leaked out from his body, the wound a gaping hole, he'd truly believed he was dying. Him! An immortal being! It wasn't supposed to be possible; he was eternal. But he'd been bested by a remnant. And now he was left wondering what would have happened to him if Emma hadn't intervened, if she hadn't saved his life. She'd pushed him away, she'd forced him to relocate, his free will had been taken from him because when Emma compelled him to do something, he had to do it. And that still smarted, but if she hadn't, would he have died?

As he'd stood, fully reformed and dressed in his preferred attire, facing the ocean with the waves lapping gently along the shoreline and the sun shining down on him, he'd felt nothing. Literally nothing, except the echoes of pain and a paralysing fear that had crept into his soul, slithered through his spirit, and taken root in his body by latching onto his heart.

"Blake," Emma mumbled, rousing him from his deliberations. "Why don't you get into bed with me?"

"You need your sleep," Blake replied, surprised that she'd woken without him realising.

"I can't sleep while you're drowning in fear. Come to bed. Let's talk about it."

"I don't want to talk about it."

Emma sighed quietly, threw back the covers, and padded to the bathroom. On her return, she took hold of Blake's hand and pulled him into bed with her, despite the fact that he was fully clothed. "Most people are afraid of something, Blake. You know that. You can feel what I feel."

"You've had a lot to deal with recently."

"You've had a lot to deal with too," Emma replied, and then paused. Blake sensed that she expected him to reply, but he didn't. He didn't know what to say. Eventually she carried on speaking. "Very few people live a life without fear, you know. We worry about the people we love; we worry that we're not living our best lives; hell, we even worry that we've got nothing to wear."

Blake knew that Emma had added her last point only to lighten the mood, but he still chose to answer only that. "You have a wardrobe full of clothes."

"And I've still got nothing to wear," Emma deadpanned. "My

point is that anxiety is a part of our everyday lives; it's part of being human."

"I'm not worried or anxious."

"No, you're terrified. I can feel it. Worry, anxiety, fear… they're all related, but they're not exactly the same. I'm not explaining myself very well, am I? It is the middle of the night after all!" She huffed before continuing. "I'm not trying to trivialise what you're going through, Blake, but you need to deal with it."

"How did you get over it?"

"Get over what?" Emma asked before realising what Blake meant. "Oh, that!" She chuckled. "I got angry."

"I've been angry all my life."

"I know, and I'm not saying that you have to get angry. Everybody has a different coping mechanism, a different way of conquering their fears. Some people believe in facing them head-on. Some people believe in laughing at them. What you shouldn't do, what you can't do, is hide from them. I tried that, didn't I? I hid out here. I barely went out. All I did was cut myself off from the people I love, the people who wanted to help me."

"Peter is dead. You have nothing to fear."

"Anais is dead."

"But… it's not the same."

"Isn't it?"

"No, it's different."

"It's exactly the same. You need to move past it. You need to let it go."

"You still think about what Joanne did."

"You're right, I do. But it doesn't stop me from getting on with my life. It didn't stop me from going to Ellie's today, it didn't stop me from helping her decorate her apartment, and it isn't going to stop me from being happy for her. You can do this, Blake. I know you can."

"I'll think about it," Blake replied, pulling Emma closer into him, effectively closing down the conversation. A hush descended on the room, engulfing it whole. Only the quiet, contented little snores of Cooper and Watson—Emma's two little cats—could be heard for a while. In time Emma drifted back off to sleep, but Blake remained awake, holding her in his arms, processing what she'd said, trying to work through his emotions, emotions that were all brand new to him.

Chapter 5 – Emma
Thursday 30th May 2019 / Friday 31st May 2019

    Blake and I spent a cosy few days at home after our heart-to-heart. We didn't really do anything, but we talked and we laughed. Well, I laughed. I was starting to think that Blake was physically incapable of laughing. I did however manage to get a smile out of him on more than one occasion, and I was taking that to be progress. After all, Blake was never going to be the life and soul of a party.

    We purposely didn't talk about what had happened in the last few weeks, and we stayed away from topics that related to the prophecy. Essentially we dated, but we didn't leave the house, opting for home-cooked meals or takeout.

    "Okay, I'm going to teach you how to make a lasagne," I announced as dinnertime approached on the third day.

    "I have to cook tea?" Blake trailed after me into the kitchen.

    "Yes, you do. If you want to be a real live boy, then you need to experience all that life has to offer, including chores. Anyway, I think you'd make an excellent chef. You must have reaped some amazing ones over the years. You could borrow their recipes."

    "No one stands out."

    "Has anyone ever stood out?" I asked, intrigued. Blake must have reaped hundreds of thousands of people from all walks of life. Royalty, celebrities, politicians, criminals…

    "Only Alice Elizabeth Edwards."

    "Grammy?" I stopped what I was doing and turned to stare at Blake because of course I recognised the name immediately. Grammy had been Ellie's maternal grandmother, but she'd been as much my Grammy as she'd been Ellie's. She'd died around about the time that Peter had attacked me, so not that long ago.

    "She's the only one who's ever known about me."

    "But… that's not right. Grandpa Harold told her about you. At the very least, he knew about you."

    "I've never shown up in anyone else's memories. Before you, no one has ever seen me, heard me, talked about me, or written about me."

"I don't understand." I was puzzled. I'd caught on quite quickly to what was bothering Blake. "You *did* reap Grandpa Harold's soul, didn't you?"

"I did. And while we know that he knew about me, there wasn't any reference to me in his memories. How's that possible?"

I tilted my head, confused. Blake was right—how was that possible? "That's a really good question," I remarked, more to myself than to Blake. "Maybe people can keep things from you when you reap their souls," I suggested.

"No, Emma, they can't. They're dead. They don't have any control over the process. I administer the Kiss of Death, and in doing so, I watch their life unfold. I don't always pay attention, but the memories remain with me." Blake spoke to me as if I were a child and he was having to explain something for the fifty-ninth time.

"Have you tried looking through them again?"

"I have. Harold doesn't once mention the Keeper of Souls. No one does. Plenty of people talk about the Grim Reaper, but no one, other than Alice, has ever said anything about me."

"But Grammy learned about you from Grandpa Harold," I insisted.

"I know."

"Can you find the corresponding memories in each of them?"

Blake didn't answer, but a faint frown crossed his face. I assumed he was doing whatever it was that he did when he wanted to revisit someone else's memories, and so I got on with getting out what we would need for the innards of the lasagne: beef mince, onions, passata, garlic, herbs, and some sugar. And yes, I know that sugar might sound like an odd choice of ingredient for a lasagne, but it takes away the bitterness of the tomatoes.

"Can you chop while you're doing that?" I asked.

"No," Blake replied, "but I'm done." His frown had deepened.

"Well?"

"Well, what?"

I clenched my jaw tightly shut and counted to ten before speaking. "Did you find anything?"

"No," Blake answered. "The memories that Alice had of Harold telling her about me simply don't exist in Harold."

"What? Not at all?" I asked, placing a chopping board, a knife, and the onion in front of Blake. "Top and tail that and then cut it in half," I directed.

Absently—and somewhat surprisingly—Blake did as I instructed.

"Now peel off the skin and then dice the rest of the onion," I carried on, leaving Blake to chop while I dug out the frying pan. When I straightened up, Blake was scowling at me, but the onion had been shredded. "What?"

"My eyes are stinging," Blake snapped.

Laughter bubbled up inside of me, slipping out before I could clamp my mouth shut. I felt helpless, unable to hold it in. Blake's eyes were indeed rimmed red and filled with tears. "Whatever you do, don't rub them," I told him. "You'll make it worse."

"You knew this would happen."

"No, I didn't. It depends on the strength of the onion, as I'm sure you know full well if you stop and think about it." I chuckled again, surrendering to the feeling of mirth before giving my next instruction. "Okay, you want to put the mince and the onion into the frying pan and cook them together on a low heat until the mince is brown and the onion has softened." With a degree of effort, I schooled my face into a more serious expression.

"Why do I have to make tea anyway?" Blake continued to stare at me.

"Because I'm a modern woman, and I have absolutely no intention of doing all the cooking and cleaning for the rest of my life. If you want to be a part of my life, you'll have to do your fair share."

An electric charge ran through my body. Blake's emotions had just spiked. "You're planning a life for us?"

"Aren't you?"

"I try not to think about the future," he admitted.

"It's scary, isn't it?" I sighed, the joy I'd felt only moments ago draining away. "I'll grow old and die, leaving you on your own again."

"Yes."

"But we have now, Blake." I took a step towards him and took his hands in mine. "And I love you with all my heart. I fully intend on enjoying whatever time we have together."

"By making me do chores," Blake answered, despite the waves

of emotion that were pulsing out of him and sweeping over me.

"That's a part of it, yes." I stepped closer still and pressed my body into his.

"You've never said you love me before." Blake acknowledged my declaration at last.

"No, I haven't. I should have done. I should have said 'I love you too' when you first said it to me, but I was overwhelmed at the time, and then everything went a little crazy. I've been waiting for the perfect moment ever since, but I've just realised that there is no perfect moment, there's only now." I gazed into Blake's eyes. They were such a dark brown that they could almost have been described as black.

Blake hummed a reply before leaning in to place the gentlest of kisses on the tip of my nose, and then his lips searched out mine. It was a while before we returned to the task of cooking our dinner.

Telling Blake that I loved him deepened our relationship somehow. It was a difficult thing to explain, but there was a security there that had been missing before. The tension drained out of us both; we were happier just to be with each other, to sit in silence. I'd known that I'd been in love with Blake for weeks, so why hadn't I said it before now? Why hadn't I given him that most precious of gifts? He'd known of course, not only could we feel each others' emotions, but Blake could listen in to all of my internal chatter. There had been no hiding it from him. He knew that I loved him before I knew that I loved him, but there's nothing quite like hearing those all-important words, is there? And in the end, I was glad I'd told him when I did because the very next day, while I was en route home from Cedar's Veterinary Centre, my life went to shit for the third time since meeting Blake.

The drive from Cedar's Veterinary Centre to my house was not a lengthy one. It was as simple as turning right out of the practice, turning right again onto the main road (although calling it a main road was a bit of a stretch), and following the aforementioned 'main' road through the countryside for a couple of miles to the edge of the village that I called home. There were various routes through the village to where I actually lived, the street on which my little two-up two-down could be found, the one that petered out into nothing. But, being a creature of habit, I usually drove through the market square, past the mini-market and a Chinese takeaway, and finally past the chippy. It was all very handy for when I needed to stop off for a pint of milk or if I couldn't be bothered cooking.

My heart was so full of joy the day after I'd told Blake that I loved him, that I was already singing along to the radio as I exited Cedar's car park. And then I spun the wheel of my beloved sunshine yellow Juke (which had taken a bit of a battering when Peter had attacked me but which had been fully restored since) to turn onto the main road. After that, it all went to pot quite quickly. And no, it wasn't my singing that was to blame, even if it was a little off-key and I didn't exactly get the words out right. Somehow, I doubted that anyone's 'vision of love' only wore socks and gloves. It was a good job that what I lacked in talent, I made up for in enthusiasm. I belted out my made-up song lyrics quite happily. Life was good. In fact, life was better than good. I loved Blake, he loved me, and we were happy together. True, not everything was perfect, but we were working on putting all of the crap that had happened behind us, and although there was still that pesky little prophecy to be dealt with, nothing untoward had happened for a while.

You know what they say about people who get too comfortable though. That's when the Sword of Damocles falls.

I'd barely done a mile on the main road when I spied a car parked up ahead with its bonnet up. I was no expert on cars, but from a distance, it looked like Charlotte's. Or Matthew's. Despite being unrelated, they drove identical cars: same make, same model, and even the same dark blue colour. Of course, it could have been anyone's car, but logic suggested that it was Charlotte's car because she'd left the practice moments before me. Or Matthew's because he'd left at around about the same time. Mind you, I assumed it was Charlotte's, which was terribly sexist of me, wasn't it?

Fleetingly, I debated simply driving past whoever it was that was stranded. At the end of the day, what could I possibly do to help? I knew less than nothing about cars. I certainly didn't know how to repair one. And surely whoever it was would have a mobile phone of their own to ring for a pickup. But it just didn't seem right leaving Charlotte (or Matthew!) on their own, assuming it was one of the two of them.

I pulled in behind the dark blue saloon, cut the engine of my car, unclipped my seat belt, and pushed open my car door. Whoever was stranded had chosen to remain sitting in their vehicle while they waited for their pickup, even though that went against the normal advice given.

I slid from my car, slamming the door shut behind me, and sauntered over, fully expecting to find Charlotte behind the wheel.

"Hello." It was Matthew who emerged from the car. "Fancy meeting you here," he remarked, running a hand through his hair, a myriad of woven bracelets slipping down his wrist.

"Indeed, what are the odds?" I laughed. "I take it that you've rung for help already." I nodded my head towards his car.

"No, there's no need," he replied, taking a step closer to me, pulling a white handkerchief from the pocket of his chinos.

"Really, do you know what's wrong with it then?" I asked. Maybe it was a simple fix. Or maybe he'd pulled over to make a phone call. Or read a book. I had glimpsed a number of old leather-bound books scattered on the passenger seat of his car. But then again, if that was the case, why was his bonnet up?

"Nothing's wrong with it. I was hoping you'd stop."

"Really? What if I hadn't?" I frowned at Matthew, bewildered. He wasn't making any sense. Why would he want me to stop for him? Surely if he'd wanted something, he could have just asked me about it at work. And he knew that I had a boyfriend, so even if he had taken a fancy to me (which I very much doubted!), he wouldn't be quite so forward about it, would he?

"Yes, really. Do you find that strange?" Matthew took another step in my direction. I was starting to feel uncomfortable, crowded even, but it was Matthew. I didn't really feel like I could back away from him without coming across as being rude. I mean, it was Matthew. Matthew was the vet that all our clients loved. He was great with the animals, he had a smile for everyone, and he was quick to offer help to all and sundry.

"Well, erm…" My voice trailed off. "You're behaving a little peculiarly, Matthew," I admitted with a nervous laugh.

"Am I?" Matthew stared at me with his piercing blue eyes.

"A little. Look, if you're okay, I'd best be heading home. Blake will be expecting me," I explained, turning to leave.

"Ahhh yes, Blake," Matthew muttered. Something in his voice startled me, and I took a quick step in the direction of my own car. I didn't know what Matthew was playing at, but he was making me feel increasingly uncomfortable. "Emma, wait!" Matthew called. Instinct glued my feet to the ground, and I turned to see what Matthew wanted, presuming he was going to apologise. Clearly I was the butt of some kind of joke that had gone wrong. That was the only scenario that made any sense. Time stilled, jerking me from one moment to the next, from one sensation to the next.

The tickle of cotton against my nose.

The sweet smell of some kind of drug.

An icy cold sensation in my lungs.

The snap of a lock clicking shut.

The cold feel of metal against my wrists.

And then my world went black for the second time in a week.

At least I came round in my own head relatively quickly this time, or at least I thought I did. Time had lost all meaning.

"What's happening?" I jerked upright.

"They've come for you," Johnna answered, or at least I guessed it was Johnna (who else would it be?), but panic had stripped me of rational thought. My heart was beating too fast, and my breathing felt laboured. "We always knew they would."

"They? Who's they? And who are you? Is that you, Johnna?"

"It's me, child. I told you that I'd always be here for you," she paused before going on to state the bleeding obvious. "You really do need to calm down, my dear. Hyperventilating isn't going to do you any good. Come on, deep breaths." I peered into the unending gloom and thought I saw a familiar outline. My mind filled in the blanks and, rightly or wrongly, decided that Johnna was demonstrating some deep breathing exercises. She was sitting with her legs crossed, and with each intake of breath, she lifted her hands towards her face, letting them fall back down to her lap as she exhaled. Maybe I only imagined it, but what she said made sense, so I mimicked her movements.

"Johnna," I eventually replied, my voice a little breathy still. "I don't understand what's going on."

"You've been kidnapped."

"Kidnapped?!"

"That's right." Johanna didn't seem all that bothered by what was happening, but my heart was still racing despite the breathing exercises.

"By who?"

"By a group of people who want to use you."

"Use me? To do what?"

"I thought you'd been paying attention. They want you to open a portal into Hell."

"I don't know how to do that."

"You can compel Blake to do anything… anything at all."

I had no answer to that because I knew that Johnna was right. I *could* force Blake to do anything that I wanted; I'd done it before. "But… it was Matthew," I said.

"And?"

"I like Matthew," I replied, my voice small. Johnna didn't answer, so eventually I asked another question. "What am I going to do?"

"There isn't much you can do at the minute, my dear. It's up to Ellie now."

"Ellie?"

"Yes, you've read the prophecy."

"I've *seen* the prophecy," I corrected. "No one's read it. It's written in an old angelic script. Even Blake can't read it."

"Abaddon can read it; she wrote it."

"But Abaddon isn't exactly on our side."

"You might find that Abaddon surprises you when the time comes."

"We can't even get in touch with her."

"She'll come when she's needed. Have a little faith."

Despite the feeling of panic that still threatened to overwhelm me, I rolled my eyes, hoping that Johnna wouldn't see me—we were in my own personal black hole after all. "If you say so," I deadpanned before asking if she knew what the prophecy said.

"*Behold!*" Johnna's voice echoed in the empty space. *"That which was torn asunder will be reunited in the light of a new moon. The golden soul will be as it once was, and all will be as it should have been. Order and balance will be restored. And in the days that follow, the beast will be set free."*

"That doesn't say that Ellie's it."

Johnna tutted. "I haven't finished yet," she said before continuing on with her recital of the prophecy. "*Guard well the one with angel blood running through her veins, for she will decide which of the beasts is to be called forth. Her actions, and her actions alone, will dictate if the in-between becomes a battleground once more or if peace and harmony will reign for all time. Wait patiently until she is born, and know her by her real name, the shining light.*"

"That still doesn't say that Ellie's it."

"And if I tell you that Eleanor means 'shining light'?"

"Holy sh—" I started to say.

"There's no need for that kind of language in here, my dear."

"Aren't we in my head?"

"Technically yes, but I've occupied this space for longer than you've known about it, so we'll play by my rules if you don't mind."

I bit my lip before opening my mouth to speak again. "That passage… what if one of the guardians before Ellie had been named Eleanor?" It felt odd calling Ellie by her given name. No one ever did; she was always just Ellie.

"None of the others have been called Eleanor."

"But what if Grandpa Harold had wanted Joanne to be called Eleanor."

"He didn't though. The time wasn't right."

"But, what if—"

"Emma," Johnna interrupted. "I know your generation likes to play the what-if game, but you need to accept that only when the time was right would a guardian be named Eleanor."

"Fine," I mumbled before another question occurred. "How do you know what the prophecy says? If you're like me and you didn't know about Blake until after you died, how's it possible that you've learned about the prophecy? Surely you only know what I know."

Johnna tutted, not even trying to hide her dismay at my ignorance. "The problem with you and Blake is that you're each only half of a whole," she said, not even bothering to answer my question. Or at least if that was her answer, I didn't understand it.

"Sooo…?" I prompted, still wanting to understand how Johnna knew what the prophecy said.

Johnna glared at me before elaborating further. "The golden soul is unchanging."

"And?"

"And John held it once."

I shrugged, still not getting what Johnna was trying to tell me, but she made no effort to go into any more detail. "Well, if you won't tell me how you know what the prophecy says, will you at least tell me who 'they' are?" I reached up into the darkness to insert the air quotes.

I felt, rather than saw, Johnna shudder beside me. "They're an ancient order of demon worshippers. They've been waiting for the Key to meet with the Keeper of Souls so that they can perform a ritual on her, one that they believe will fuse the soul back together again."

"And open the portal?" I surmised.

"And open the portal," Johnna confirmed.

"How do I stop them?"

"As I said once before, dear, you need to remember to use the power of your ancestors when the time is right."

Chapter 6 – Blake
Friday 31st May 2019

Blake settled so that it looked like he was sitting on the sofa next to where Cooper was sprawled out on a blanket. It seemed impossible for the little black cat to curl up in the same way that Watson did, but he'd done his best, wrapping his thick, muscular tail around his body, the tip of it covering his nose.

Blake reached out with his left hand and imagined what it would feel like to stroke Cooper's fur. Cooper's ears twitched, even though Blake knew that he hadn't actually touched him, just as he wasn't actually sitting on the sofa. He glanced up at the newly installed wrought-iron clock. The hands had barely inched forwards, even though it felt like hours had passed since he'd last checked the time. Emma had put the clock up for him only last week. He'd gone to her workplace on more than one occasion, wanting to know when she was coming home. After venting at him, she'd eventually realised that he was unable to tell the time without her in the house. It wasn't that he didn't know how to, it was that everything in her home that marked the passage of time required a button press. Of course, he could translocate himself to somewhere else; England was littered with churches and many of them had a clock tower, but he didn't like to leave Emma's home. Her scent lingered in the air and, while he knew that he couldn't perceive it, or touch any of her belongings, being there made him feel better.

Finally, six o'clock rolled around. Emma would be home within the next half hour. On one occasion, he'd translocated himself into her car while she'd been en route home. It hadn't gone as he'd thought it might. Emma, despite being used to him arbitrarily appearing out of thin air, had been shocked by his presence. She'd jerked the wheel of her car, very nearly plunging them headfirst into oncoming traffic. After a lecture on road safety, he'd been instructed to wait for her at home on the days that she had to work.

Feeling antsy, Blake stood and began pacing from one end of the house to the other. If he'd have needed to avoid the furniture, he'd have only managed two or three paces in either direction, but he didn't need to avoid the furniture. Instead, he strode from the front room window to the back patio doors before turning on his heel and returning to the front room window. Seven times he paced from one end of the house to the other and back again, twenty-nine times, eighty-three… a hundred… 142. He looked at the clock again and saw that it was finally after half six. Emma should be home by now, but perhaps she'd got caught up in something, or perhaps she'd stopped at the shop. She had no way of letting him know if that was the case. Cedar's wasn't all that far away, but it was far enough to interfere with their telepathic link, and Blake couldn't use a phone.

Blake stopped his pacing and literally stood watching the clock, facing it square on. Seven o'clock rolled around and a new kind of fear slowly unfurled itself within him, threading itself through his heart, taking a choke hold on his throat.

Emma was most definitely not dead. Blake would know if she was, he'd have reaped her soul. Not only that, he would have known if the possibility of death had been in her future. That was one of his gifts: he could sense the likelihood of someone dying in the near term. No, she was most definitely not dead, but if she wasn't dead, where was she?

With nothing more than an idle thought, Blake relocated to Emma's workplace, Cedar's Veterinary Centre. The car park was empty; everyone had left for the day, everyone including Emma. Just to be sure, Blake checked inside the building. The reception area, the treatment rooms, the room for the overnighters… all were empty, except for Jessica and Fletcher, who were curled up together in the staff room. It was almost impossible to tell where one kitten ended and the other started, legs and tails were wrapped around each other, and ginger fur was entangled with ginger fluff. Blake stood watching them for a moment. They didn't snore like Cooper and Watson, but they were clearly contented. Blake continued with his search anyway, looking upstairs, searching for signs of life or of anything amiss. Nothing was out of place. Andrew's office looked like it had been ransacked—papers were scattered everywhere, and books were piled on top of more books—but that was perfectly normal.

Returning to the car park, Blake called for Seith, the only companion he'd ever known until he'd met Emma. "Emma has disappeared," he announced the second that Seith appeared. "Yes, I'm sure," he continued after Seith had sought confirmation. "She's gone." Blake spoke calmly, but he was in turmoil. His worst nightmare had come true. He'd never felt such despair, not even when Emma had been attacked. That had happened so quickly, it had been over before he'd had time to feel anything. But this… this… it was all-consuming. A single thought dominated his mind: where was Emma?

Seith barked, forcing Blake to focus on the present.

"Yes, do that," Blake commanded. He watched as Seith rose and trotted from the car park, exiting right, following the route that Emma would have taken if she'd returned home.

Blake's fear rooted his feet to the floor; he wasn't sure what to do. Should he return to Emma's house or stay where he was? Should he follow Seith or search somewhere else? Blake didn't know. He'd never been able to pinpoint Emma's location, and while she could always pull him to her, he couldn't pull her to him. Her ability relied on the fact that he was mostly incorporeal and could therefore be pulled through space.

Time slowed down. Blake became acutely aware of the distant sounds of traffic. Birds sang cheerfully in the trees and bushes nearby. Together, the two formed a new noise, a roaring in his ears. And then Seith howled, a mournful howl filled with pain and suffering. Blake relocated again. Emma's car had been neatly parked at the side of the road, but Emma was nowhere to be found. Blake's knees simply gave way and he crumpled to the ground. He just knew that something had happened to her, but she wasn't dead. He held on tightly to that one thought. Emma. Wasn't. Dead.

Chapter 7 – Ellie
Friday 31st May 2019

Early evening sunlight flooded Ellie's apartment, giving it a cheery glow. It had been almost a week since she'd moved in, and the place was finally starting to feel like home. After the painting party, with Scott's help, she'd finished off the decorating and unpacked her belongings.

The bedroom was now a pale lemon colour. The bed had been made up with some crisp white bedding, a lilac throw, and some patterned scatter cushions. Curtains had been hung at the windows, and a lamp had been placed on the bedside table. When it was turned on, it made the room look nice and cosy. All in all, the room looked as neat as a pin.

The lounge was a rich honey colour, and in deference to what had happened there, the furniture had been moved around. The sofa, which had once faced into the room, now faced outwards, which worked because the view really was rather nice. A burnt orange blanket had been hung over the back of the sofa, and some more scatter cushions brought the colours of the bedroom into the lounge. There was no escaping the fact that it was the same sofa it had always been, but underneath the mounds of soft furnishings, it now looked quite inviting.

Scott had built a flat-pack television unit and tucked it into the corner of the lounge, next to the bedroom wall. He'd put a bookcase in the dining room so that Ellie had space for some knick-knacks, and he'd made her a wrought-iron coat rack that was now screwed to the wall by the front door. Because the apartment was mostly open plan, there wasn't that much wall space for pictures but Ellie had put one up. It showed a single sunflower superimposed over a page from her favourite book.

The kitchen and the bathroom were exactly as Joanne had left them. The kitchen had creamy-coloured units with an oak worktop, and the bathroom had a simple white suite, with square white tiles on the walls.

Moving the furniture around had made the space feel different, changing the colour of the walls had brightened the place up a bit, and unpacking her clothes had given Ellie a sense of belonging, but most of all Scott's presence had kept the smile on her face. He was yet to be persuaded of all that he'd learned in the past few days—and there had been many long conversations. It wasn't that he didn't believe it, per se. Instead, it was that the whole thing was so unbelievable that he was struggling to wrap his head around it. And that was understandable, wasn't it? No one in the history of mankind had ever been asked to accept that their sister was dating the Keeper of Souls and that their girlfriend had been named in an aeons-old prophecy.

Naturally, Scott had wanted to see the artefacts that had been handed down through the generations, ultimately ending up with Ellie. He'd unrolled the ancient scroll to peer at the symbols inked onto the papyrus before admiring the polished wooden handle of the angel blade. And then he'd removed the cover from the knife, exposing the pearlescent blade, which he'd promptly tested on his thumb. He didn't quite cut his hand to ribbons, but it was a close call.

"Tell me again what Abaddon said," Scott demanded, his feet up on the sofa while Ellie cooked tea.

"Again?" Ellie laughed. "I've told you about it a million times already."

"Come on," Scott wheedled, "humour me."

"Fine." Ellie huffed, but with no real annoyance. "Abaddon was waiting for me in my bedroom a few weeks ago."

"Looking like me?"

Ellie rolled her eyes. "Yes, Scott, looking like you. And for the record, your work boots will not be left to lie wherever they fall. I was hoping you'd build me a nice little shoe rack for our outdoor shoes. It would look cute over there, wouldn't it?" She waved in the direction of the front door, where Scott had put the coat rack up for her.

Scott propped himself up on his elbows and grinned at Ellie. "If you tell me what Abaddon said without getting distracted, I'll make you whatever you want."

"Okay, no distractions. As you know, Abaddon eventually introduced herself to me as an angel. She told me how Blake had come into being and that if the Key—"

"That's Emma?"

"Yes, that's Emma… if the Key was ever reunited with Blake, the Keeper of Souls, then the sh— well… the you-know-what would hit the fan."

"Because there are people who want to use Emma, forcing her to make Blake open a portal into Hell?"

"And into Heaven, I guess, but it's Hell that we're worried about because, you know… demons."

"Okay, keep going."

"Honestly, you don't really need me to tell you any of this. You know the story already."

"That's the thing, though. It isn't just a story, is it? You're really the Guardian."

Ellie shrugged. "So I'm told. Apparently Abaddon injected her blood into one of my ancestors, thus creating the line of guardians."

"And presumably she stuck around long enough to explain everything."

"Well, yes. And to hand over the artefacts."

"All of which have been passed down through the generations until your mum was supposed to give them to you."

"But she didn't because she wanted me to have a normal life. She hid the artefacts here instead, where neither me or Dad would ever stumble over them."

"I still can't believe she kept all of this from you, from your dad."

"Me either, but apparently the guardians are sworn to secrecy. Grandpa Harold was the only one who's ever broken the rules."

"As far as you know."

"Huh?"

"Well, it's possible that there have been other guardians who've told people what they knew."

"I guess." Ellie shrugged again. "Anyway, now I have to stop a horde of demons from descending on Earth. Abaddon said that I need to kill Emma to stop her from being used in the ritual, but, as even she pointed out, that's not really a solution because souls are passed down through the generations of families. Eventually Emma's soul would be reborn, and the baby would be used in the ritual instead."

"But I thought the two halves of the soul had to meet before

Emma's half could be used to call for Blake."

"They did. Abaddon explained that that was a fail-safe of sorts. But they have met; Blake knows about the soul now. If Emma were to die, when the soul was reborn, he wouldn't stay away."

"Okay, I get that. I think."

"Abaddon's alternative solution is that I kill Emma and have the soul cleaved instead of reaped."

"How's that any different?"

"As I understand it, when Blake reaps a soul, he takes it into himself until it can be reborn. But when he uses the scythe on one, it's destroyed, it ceases to exist."

Scott sighed loudly, slumping back onto the sofa. "I wish I'd thought on and asked Blake to show me his scythe."

"I don't think that would have gone down very well. He's a bit possessive about it. Besides which, you did enough damage to yourself with the angel blade."

Scott winced and glanced down at his hand, which was still healing after he'd 'tested' the angel blade. "Have you seen it? The scythe, I mean. What's it like?"

"Massive," Ellie replied.

"This is so messed up."

"Yep."

"And you don't know what the prophecy says?"

"Nope. Well, that's not entirely true. I know a little snippet of it, and I know that it says I'm it." Ellie paused, focussed for a moment on dishing up the tea that she'd cooked while she and Scott had been talking, chilli-con-carne topped off with grated cheese. "Dinner's ready," she announced before carrying a bowl of food to Scott, who quickly sat up straight on the sofa.

"Mmm, this smells so good," Scott said, leaning over his dinner and inhaling deeply, a smile on his face.

"It's quick and easy after work," Ellie replied, returning to the kitchen. Luckily, she hadn't quite picked up her own bowl when Blake appeared. "Blake!" she gasped, her bowl dropping back onto the kitchen counter with a thunk. "What on Earth are you doing here?"

"What's going on?" Scott asked, twisting in his seat to look over his shoulder in Ellie's direction.

"Emma's missing," Blake announced.

"What do you mean she's missing? I got a text from her a couple of minutes ago."

"Ellie, what's going on?" Scott asked again.

"She texted you?" The tension drained from Blake's shoulders. "She's okay. Where is she?"

"Ellie!" Scott interjected sharply.

"Oh dammit, you can't see Blake, can you?" Ellie finally replied to Scott.

"Blake's here?"

"Yes, he says Emma's missing, but she texted me a couple of minutes ago. Mind you," Ellie paused, thinking about the text, "she was quite curt."

"Curt how?" Blake asked.

"Hold on, I'll read it to you. Let me just get my phone." Ellie reached across the kitchen counter, dinner forgotten.

The thirty seconds that it took Ellie to retrieve and unlock her phone were thirty seconds too many for Blake. He stood still, apparently waiting patiently, but he didn't quite manage to wipe the scowl from his face.

"Here we go." Ellie heaved a sigh of relief. "It says, *not feeling well, going to bed, speak soon.*"

"Wait a second," Scott interrupted before Blake could reply. He jumped to his feet, his own dinner abandoned on the floor, and rooted around in his pocket until he found his phone. "She sent a group text to me, Mum, and Dad, and it didn't say anything of the sort."

"What did your text say then?" Ellie asked, frowning.

"It said, *hi Mum, hi Dad, Blake and I have decided to go away for a few days. I'm not on duty again until after the weekend. Will one of you feed Cooper and Watson for me, please?*" Scott looked up before adding, "Dad replied, but I didn't bother."

"What did your dad say?" Ellie closed the gap between her and Scott to have a look at his phone.

"You know Dad. He said, *okay, love Dad.*"

Ellie took Scott's phone and scrolled through the group chat. "That's odd," she remarked, glancing up to look at Blake, who'd not moved a muscle since appearing. "Emma hasn't put any kisses at the end of this text." She looked back at her own phone. "She didn't put any kisses at the end of the text to me either."

"What's odd about that?" Scott asked.

"Emma ends every single text message the same way. She always signs off with two little x's. She never misses them off, not even when she's texting Andrew about a work issue." Ellie paused before adding, "And, now that I think about it, Emma doesn't have another day off tomorrow. She's just had four days off in a row."

"I told you," Blake declared. "Emma's missing."

"It does look that way, doesn't it?" Ellie absently passed Scott's phone back to him. Her frown deepened. She couldn't quite comprehend the severity of the situation. Only moments before she'd been about to sit down and have dinner with Scott, but now Emma was missing. How did that happen so suddenly?

"What are we going to do about it?" Blake asked, interrupting Ellie's bewildered musings.

"Erm… I don't know. Perhaps you'd better sit down."

Blake didn't answer. Instead, he strode through Ellie's apartment, taking the most direct route from where he'd appeared to stand by the window, passing harmlessly through the sofa, before glaring at Ellie.

"Oh, of course. I forgot, sorry."

"What did you forget? What just happened?" Scott asked.

"Blake is only whole…" Ellie started to say before catching sight of Blake's face. Spitting cobras looked happier than he did. "…erm, corporeal when he's near Emma. That's why he vanished the other day, remember? Emma stepped too far away from him. And to prove his point," Ellie tilted her head and raised her eyebrows, "he just walked through the furniture."

"Oh, where is he now? I don't want to sit on him."

"You won't. He's standing by the window," Ellie reassured Scott, gently guiding him back towards the sofa before perching at the other end. "Is this real? Emma's really missing?" she asked, the truth of what had happened suddenly dawning on her. "We should call the police, shouldn't we? What actually happened, Blake? How do you know Emma's missing? The texts could be someone playing games, couldn't they?"

"She's missing," Blake answered. "She didn't come home from work. I waited until seven o'clock and then I searched Cedar's. She wasn't there, so I called for Seith."

"What's he saying?" Scott leant towards Ellie and whispered.

"Shush, I'll fill you in in a minute," Ellie answered. "Go on, what happened next? What did Seith say?"

"Seith found her car parked by the side of the road."

"Okay, that doesn't mean she's missing though. Maybe she got a flat." Ellie was grasping at straws, and she knew it, but she really didn't want Emma to be missing.

"She didn't get a flat. The car's fine. She's missing."

"Shit!" Ellie muttered, leaning forwards and gently bouncing one of her legs. "Where's Seith now?"

"Out searching still."

Ellie paled. "This is real, isn't it? What are we going to do?"

Scott reached over and laid a hand on Ellie's thigh, surmising some of what Blake had said. "First of all, we'll ring Mum and Dad and then we'll ring the police. It's okay. They'll find her."

"No, Scott. No, they won't." Ellie shook her head, tears welling up in her eyes. "The police won't be able to do anything about this. This is it, isn't it? The prophecy's coming true." Ellie looked at Blake, but Blake only shrugged. "Can't you sense her?" she asked.

"No."

"But—"

"I can sense her emotions and hear her thoughts when I'm close enough to her, but I can't pinpoint her location. I've never been able to do that. And I can't pull her to me in the same way that she can pull me to her."

"So, we're buggered then?"

"What did Blake say?" Scott asked, forcing Ellie to relay Blake's half of the conversation.

"We need Abaddon," Blake suddenly announced. "She knows what the prophecy says, she can help us find Emma."

"But we don't know how to get in touch with her."

"I know how to get in touch with her," Blake's expression was grim, "but it will require a sacrifice on your behalf."

Ellie swallowed hard before answering. "Anything for Emma."

Chapter 8 – Ellie
Friday 31st May 2019

"Do you really think this will work?" Ellie asked, looking up at Blake.

"Think what will work?" Scott sounded frustrated.

"Blake thinks that if he attacks me with the scythe, then Abaddon will show up," Ellie explained in a matter-of-fact way. She could just as easily have been explaining how to turn the pages of a book.

"WHAT?! No way." Scott jumped up from the sofa and turned towards where he thought Blake was standing, angling his body ready for a fight. "This," he jabbed his fingers belligerently in the air, "is not happening. You will not harm a hair on Ellie's head," he stated. His brow was furrowed, and his chin was tilted downwards. He meant business. But because blood had surged into his face, he looked like an angry comic book character complete with red hair and ruddy-coloured features. All he needed to do was clench his fists and stamp his feet and then the look would be complete.

"You can't stop him even if you wanted to," Ellie answered, still sitting on the sofa, "and Blake's not standing there anymore." Worry lines were etched into her forehead.

Scott glanced at her before answering, "Well, where is he? Has he gone?"

"Tell him I'm still here," Blake said before Ellie could answer Scott herself. "Tell him that no one will stop me from doing whatever needs to be done in order to save his sister. And tell him that if he doesn't pipe down, I'll tell Emma all about a certain conversation he had with Alice when he was seven."

"What conversation between Scott and Grammy?" Ellie asked. Despite the circumstances, or maybe because of them, she couldn't help but be intrigued by such an anomalous titbit in the conversation.

Blake didn't answer her question. All he said was 'tell him.'

Ellie twisted in her seat to face Scott. "Blake says that if you don't pipe down—those were his words and not mine, by the way—he's going to tell Emma about a conversation that you had with Grammy when you were seven. What conversation is he on about, Scott?"

Scott paled and took a step back towards the safety of the sofa. "He wouldn't," he exclaimed while Blake prompted Ellie to repeat everything else that he'd had to say.

Ellie huffed loudly. "He also said that no one will stop him from saving Emma. And he's right," Ellie stood and slid her hand into Scott's, the conversation between him and Grammy temporarily forgotten, "no one can stop him. And I don't want to anyway. I want to help him find her."

Scott ran a hand through his hair. "Shit, me too. Of course I want to find her too." He sighed. "How the hell are we going to tell Mum and Dad? Dad is going to go nuts."

"Let's try and get hold of Abaddon first," Ellie replied. "And then we'll ring your mum and dad and then the police."

"Okay, yes." Scott nodded. Ellie surmised that he liked having a plan. "But what exactly does Blake intend to do to you?" Scott asked, somewhat mollified.

"That's a good question." Ellie looked at Blake. "Well?"

"I don't even know if it will work; my weapon has only ever been used on souls before."

"What will work?"

Blake scowled before answering. Ellie sensed that Blake was not happy about being challenged, but he did answer her. "Abaddon said that she's fond of your line. She said that she'd be displeased if anything were to happen to it. She was talking about Joanne at the time, but I think if I threaten you somehow she'll know and she'll come here to try and stop me. The only problem is that I think I'll have to draw blood to attract her attention, and I don't know if the scythe can be used on living flesh or if it is incorporeal like me."

Ellie gulped. Her mouth had suddenly gone very dry. "You used it in Charlotte's bathroom." She forced the words out.

Blake nodded once. "Maybe this will work then. It's got to. We need to speak to Abaddon."

"What will work?" Scott repeated Ellie's question. "I want to know what the plan is before anyone does anything."

"Just how much blood are we talking about, Blake?" Ellie asked, not exactly ignoring Scott but wanting all the details before she relayed the plan.

"Blood!" Scott gasped.

"I am assuming a drop, a scratch will do," Blake answered.

"Okay…" Ellie took a deep breath and then repeated herself. "Okay," she said more firmly. "Scott, I'm going to hold out my hand, and Blake is going to prick my finger."

"That's it?" Scott raised an eyebrow.

"That's it," Ellie confirmed.

"For now," Blake added ominously, not that Scott heard him.

Despite Blake's less than encouraging words, Ellie steeled herself and lifted her hand into the air, palm upwards. Naturally, she offered up her dominant hand, her right hand, but before Blake could react, she jerked it back to her side. "Wait! Perhaps we should use my left hand? Just in case."

"In case of what?" Scott asked.

"In case Blake slips." Ellie glanced at Scott and smiled briefly. "I saw how much damage you did to yourself with the angel blade after all," she added, desperately trying to lighten the mood.

"I do not slip," Blake spat, pulling his scythe from the ether. Its metal blade immediately caught the natural evening light streaming in through the windows and scattered it to the four corners of the room. Reflections danced on the wall, reflections that even Scott could see. He gazed around the room in wonder, momentarily distracted by what was going on around him.

Blake tilted the scythe so that he could hold its wooden pole with both hands diagonally across his body. The blade curved around him, its point out front. He looked straight into Ellie's icy blue eyes. Fear was stamped all over her face, her brow was furrowed, and her mouth was set in a thin, tight line. However, she held her nerve.

"Why don't you cut yourself, Ellie?" Blake suggested.

"Wha… what?" Ellie asked.

"Step forward and gently press your hand onto the blade. I won't move."

Compassion? From Blake? Ellie wondered, breathing a sigh of relief before doing as Blake had suggested. She'd barely touched the tip of the scythe's blade with her middle finger when bright red blood welled. She snatched her hand back with a hiss of pain.

"WHAT THE HELL IS GOING ON HERE?" a new voice literally screeched.

Blake didn't react. All he did was place his weapon casually back into the ether. Ellie and Scott however both jumped before turning to stare wide-eyed at the newcomer.

"Abaddon!" Ellie exclaimed. "Thank goodness you're here at last."

Abaddon ignored Ellie and Scott. She glared at Blake with such venom that if Blake hadn't been an immortal being, he'd have been dead within a second. The phrase 'if looks could kill' had never before meant so much.

"Emma is missing."

"And you thought you'd take your anger out on Ellie, did you? I told you that if you ever harmed a hair on that girl's head, your life wouldn't be worth living."

"You can't hurt me." Blake stood his ground.

"But I can hurt those you love."

"Didn't you hear me? Emma is missing."

"I am going to—"

"Abaddon, wait!" Ellie interjected. She'd finally gotten over the shocking arrival and woken up to the fact that an argument was raging in her little apartment, which was feeling very full all of a sudden. She pushed past Scott so that she could get to Abaddon. "Blake didn't hurt me. I cut myself on his scythe. We needed to speak to you."

Abaddon finally turned her attention to Ellie, her eyes narrowed into slits. "Blake didn't hurt you?"

"No. It was his idea, but I did this to myself." She lifted her hand into the air, giving Scott an opportunity to see just how badly she'd cut herself; blood was still oozing from the wound. Despite barely touching the blade, Ellie had sliced open her middle finger from its tip right down to its base.

"Why didn't you just call my name?" Abaddon asked, taking Ellie's hand in her own. A faint glow filled the room, and Ellie's flesh began knitting itself back together again. When Abaddon released Ellie's hand, all traces of blood and gore had vanished.

"Mum said that you can't be called. You only show up when you want to. That hasn't stopped me from trying, but I assumed you couldn't hear me."

"That's not true. I've always been there for your mum."

"Mum says not."

"Well, I'll admit that sometimes it took me a while to get to her. I… er… well, sometimes I was indisposed, you might say. Sometimes I had my legs wrapped around a—"

"All right, we don't need the details," Ellie interrupted.

"And once or twice it might have taken me a couple of months before I got round to checking in," Abaddon continued. "I would have gotten to you eventually; you didn't need to do this."

"Apparently I did, because it worked," Ellie stated, not pausing for breath. "Look, Abaddon, we need your help. I know that you think I should have killed Emma already, but that was never going to happen, and now she's gone missing. We need to find her before anything can happen, before she's used to get to Blake."

"Urgh." Abaddon wrinkled her nose. "Actually, I've been thinking about that and…" Her voice trailed off. She muttered something so quietly that even Ellie, who was standing closest to her, couldn't hear it.

"What was that?" Scott asked. He'd edged closer to Ellie and Abaddon while they'd been talking and was now immediately behind Ellie so that she could lean on him if she wanted to do so.

Abaddon huffed loudly before answering. "Fine," she snapped. "I don't think you killing Emma would have worked anyway. The only thing that would is a cleaving." She glanced at Blake and raised her eyebrows hopefully.

"Never."

"Hmph. That's what I thought you'd say and seeing as you're the only one who can use the flipping scythe, we're out of options."

"We're not out of options," Ellie declared. "We can rescue Emma and kill all the demons."

Abaddon started laughing.

"What? What's so funny about that?"

"Kill all the demons!" Abaddon laughed harder. She clutched at her side, gasping for breath. "Do you know how many demons there are? You can't kill them all. It would take you a lifetime."

"Fine. I can still save Emma. And then together we can find a way to make sure the portal stays closed."

"Oh, bloody hell. I guess I don't really have a choice, do I? And

I was just getting into it with a really good—"

"Do I want to know the end of that sentence?"

"What?" Abaddon asked innocently. "I was only going to say that I was just getting into it with a really good book."

"You weren't, though, were you?"

"Not at all," Abaddon sniggered.

"Urgh," Ellie sighed before nudging Scott back to the sofa so that both of them could sit down.

Blake remained where he'd been standing. "Where is she then?" he asked.

"How the hell should I know?" Abaddon answered Blake's question with one of her own.

Blake's shoulders dropped. He wilted on the spot, and his glare faded away as despair took over. If Abaddon didn't know where Emma was, what hope did he have of finding her?

"But I'll be able to find her," Abaddon added, taking pity on Blake.

Chapter 9 – Emma
Saturday 1st June 2019

Who knew how much time had passed before I was able to force my eyes open again. They stung sharply, but I resisted the urge to close them and drift back into the comforting arms of an extended slumber.

Without moving, I let my mind drift back over the events of… yesterday? Was it only yesterday or had I been unconscious for longer than that? I assumed I'd been asleep for at least one night because sunlight streamed in through a window on my left. A feeling of panic gripped me, threatening to tear apart my sanity as the memory of what had happened came flooding back. I'd been kidnapped, or at least I was fairly certain that I'd been kidnapped. I couldn't come up with any other explanation for what had happened, and believe me, I was desperately trying to think of something… anything.

I let my eyes close again, consciously taking a deep breath in, letting the air fill my lungs before exhaling slowly. And then I crow-barred my eyelids apart for a second time. If I was going to survive whatever the hell was going on, then I needed to think rationally. My prison, for want of a better word, was reasonably large and relatively well decorated. If I ignored the fact that I'd been knocked out with what I assumed was chloroform, I could almost persuade myself that I'd woken up in the luxury suite of a five-star hotel.

The place was well furnished; to my left was a smart, comfortable-looking armchair that had been positioned so as to face a television that was bolted onto the wall opposite where I lay. And to my right, there was a small chest of drawers next to the bed, and a two-person dining table in the far corner of the room. It had a couple of chairs tucked in underneath it. Perhaps I was expecting company.

There were two doors in the room. One I assumed was the exit, but where did the other one go? To a walk-in wardrobe maybe? There certainly wasn't anywhere else for clothes, not even one of those half wardrobes that you find in motels the world over. I lay there staring at the two doors for quite some time before it dawned on me. Surely the second door led to a bathroom. I certainly hoped so because now that I was a little more awake, I really needed to pee.

It took ages for me to swing my legs off the bed and stagger across the room. My head was pounding so hard that I thought my skull might split in two, and my stomach threatened to eject its contents with every step that I took. Eventually though, I made it, and while the first door didn't budge, the second one swung open with ease. Thankfully there was indeed a bathroom hiding behind it, an all-white affair, complete with a bath, toilet, and sink. What more did you need in the bathroom of a kidnapper's house? Wait! Was I even in a house? It was such an idle thought, but for some reason, it caused me to panic again. My breathing turned ragged quite quickly. What if I was in some kind of bunker that had been specifically adapted to hold me captive? And what if I wasn't even in England anymore? I mean, it wouldn't matter so much if I was in Scotland or Wales, but what if I had been transported across the sea, to Ireland or further afield? How was anyone ever going to find me if I was nowhere near home? Mind you, how was anyone ever going to find me anyway?

Blake! I screamed. The silence was deafening.

Blake! I begged again, putting every ounce of will I had into reaching him. Nothing. Nada. Zip. Loneliness washed over me. Where was Blake? He'd always come to me when I'd needed him. Why not now, when I really *really* needed him?

I'd railed against the fact that Blake could hear my thoughts when he was close by ever since I'd met him, but now I found myself desperate for our connection. I'd never before felt so alone, so isolated. I'd always been independent, strong-willed, determined to do things my own way. I'd even been happy with only myself for company, but I'd never really been alone. I'd always been surrounded by a loving family. Mum, Dad, Scott, Ellie… Ellie had been a constant presence in my life since the day I was born (well, since the day she was born because I was slightly older than her). And Blake… Blake had filled a void in my heart that I hadn't even known had existed.

My gut tied itself in knots before contracting painfully. Acting on instinct, I flew to the toilet, lifted the lid, and threw up. I hadn't eaten anything in hours, but that didn't stop my stomach from clenching over and over again until acid burned the back of my throat. Only then did I wilt. I slid down onto the floor and wrapped my arms around the toilet, like I was giving it a hug, and then I rested my head on its rim. I was overwhelmed in a way that I'd never been overwhelmed before, and sobs ripped me apart. Tears flowed unchecked, and I struggled to catch my breath because I didn't just cry, something broke inside of me and I wept.

For how long I sat on the bathroom floor embracing the toilet, I honestly couldn't say. It could have been mere moments, but equally it could have been hours. Rational thought had left the building, that is until my bladder decided it had had enough. I gave in with a final hiccupping sob. More tears threatened to fall, but I brushed them away, fighting against the despair. It was only then that I noticed a fresh set of clothes had been hung up on a hook behind the door. There was a note pinned to them. I couldn't read all of it, but it was definitely meant for me: it started with the words 'Dear Emma, please forgive…'

Forgive my ass! I thought, letting anger sweep away my misery. How dare someone—Matthew—casually steal me away from my family, my friends, my home, from Cooper and Watson, and then ask for forgiveness as if they'd done nothing more than bump into me? *Never!*

I did however want to read the rest of the note because it was nigh on impossible to ignore something that was so clearly addressed to me. I slurped a handful of water from the tap to moisten my throat, splashed some water on my face, grabbed the note, and sat back down on the toilet because, even though I'd made a real effort to finish, I needed to go again.

The note didn't actually say a great deal. I'd been hoping for a clue, but all it said was:

Dear Emma,

Please forgive the accommodation. We've done our best to make you comfortable but of course we do need to keep you secure.

Feel free to use the bathroom, take a shower if you want. You might as well, you'll be staying with us for a couple of days.

Consider the clothes a gift. With best wishes, T

It was worrying that they thought I'd be there for a few days. Now that my temper had made a resurgence, I'd started to think about escaping, as soon as I'd finished in the bathroom of course!

"At last! I see you're finally awake," Matthew remarked when I marched back into the bedroom, determined to put my plan into motion—not that I had a real plan. I'd gotten as far as thinking that I'd find something sharp or heavy, smash the window, and leg it.

Matthew's smile was so bright that you'd be forgiven for thinking I was his girlfriend, and we were on a romantic getaway together. He was certainly dressed to impress, in a smart black suit, with a black shirt and a dark red tie that was held in place by a diamond tie pin. I'd never seen him looking so sharp.

"You!" I snapped, allowing my fury to surface. I strode across the room to where he was sitting (at the dining room table) and slapped him across the face. I'd never hit anyone before. Well, I'd never hit anyone other than Scott before, and I'd never really hit him, I'd just smacked him when he'd been annoying me. But I really whacked Matthew. What I'd never thought about, what I'd never needed to think about, was how much it hurt to hit someone. The palm of my hand stung and my wrist ached from where it had been bent too far backwards, sending sharp pulses of pain up my arm. *Owww!* I whinged in the sanctuary of my own mind, resisting the urge to voice my complaint out loud, forcing myself to keep the scowl on my face.

"Feel better, do you?" Matthew asked, turning his head so that he was facing me once more. He didn't even bother to rub his cheek. He just continued to smile. "I should forewarn you that if you do that too often, or to the wrong people, they'll pump you full of drugs again."

"You drugged me?" I asked, not exactly surprised.

"Well, yes. I'm sorry about it, of course I am, but I had to get you here somehow." Matthew paused briefly before continuing. "Look, why don't you sit down? I brought you something to eat and a drink." He nodded in the direction of the table, where there was indeed a pile of food. "You must be hungry."

"Not at all," I answered, crossing my arms over my body, although my traitorous stomach chose that moment to rumble so loudly that they probably thought a thunderstorm was coming on the other side of the world, and I'd only just been sick!

"Really?" Matthew raised an eyebrow.

"I'm not eating or drinking anything of yours," I declared, despite the fact that I was actually parched.

"It's not poisoned if that's what you're thinking. They need you alive. For now, at least."

I didn't answer. I couldn't. Was I supposed to be grateful that they needed me to stay alive a little longer? They didn't *want* me alive. No, they *needed* me alive. I just stared at Matthew, a new plan starting to bubble up to the top of my consciousness.

"Ah, I get it," Matthew continued. "You think you can starve yourself to death to stop them. You can't. You haven't got enough time. All you'll do is make yourself miserable. And anyway, if they think you're sickening, they'll put you under and hook you up to an IV."

"Why? They're going to kill me anyway. Why not just get on with it?"

Matthew tilted his head. "They need to perform the ritual under the light of a new moon."

"So why nab me now? Why not wait? The new moon isn't for… I don't actually know when it is, but it's not any time soon. They must know that I'm going to do my utmost to get out of here."

"You won't succeed. Everything is bolted down in here apart from the soft furnishings. The door will be locked at all times, and the window is bulletproof. You're not getting out of here any time soon."

"But why go to all of this effort? Why not just steal me away on the night of the ritual?" What was I doing? Why was I asking Matthew about their plan? Why did it matter when they'd kidnapped me? The fact of the matter was that they'd kidnapped me.

"You need to be cleansed."

"Cleansed?" I didn't understand what Matthew was saying even though he was speaking in plain English.

"Yes, cleansed. The runes around the top of your room will ensure that you're purified ahead of the ritual." Matthew glanced up at the ceiling, and without conscious thought, I followed his gaze. I hadn't noticed earlier on, but there were indeed strange symbols painted in a dark red colour along the top of all of the walls. The red was an exact match for Matthew's tie.

"So I'm not pure enough already?" I asked sarcastically.

"Hey, if it was up to me…" Matthew's voice trailed off, and he shrugged. "The older ones though, they've been planning this for longer than I have. They want to do things by the book."

"There's a book?"

"Just who do you think they are? They're not savages, you know."

"No. Just kidnappers."

"Weeell..." Matthew tilted his head. He seemed to be saying that he could see my point, but he didn't agree.

"Are you even a vet?" I asked, not knowing where my question had come from.

"Of course I'm a vet."

"Well, that was fortunate for them."

Matthew smirked. "You think it was a coincidence that I trained to be a vet?"

I didn't answer, choosing only to shrug.

"It wasn't a coincidence." Matthew shook his head. "My entire life has been dictated by yours. I am one of the chosen ones."

"Chosen ones?"

"Yes, chosen to watch over you."

I gasped, not knowing what to say. Someone had been spying on me my entire life. I mean, I know Joanne (and Ellie, I guess) had been 'guarding' me, but this felt different, more intrusive.

"You didn't know?"

"Of course I didn't know! And why a vet? Why not a vet nurse like me?"

"Ha! In my family, we don't do anything menial. We employ people to clean up the shit. Even a vet is a bit of a step down. No, in my family, we're professionals: CEOs or lawyers. We don't do anything less."

"Menial? You think what I do is menial?" I scowled at Matthew.

"What I think doesn't matter."

"So, you what...became a vet just to get close to me?"

"Essentially yes. My family has been watching yours for generations, waiting for you to meet **him**."

"What if Andrew hadn't hired you?"

"That wasn't an option," Matthew answered with an air of confidence. "Besides, I was the perfect candidate. I had an exemplary record, and I presented myself in a way that appealed to him. You think I dressed like a bum because I wanted to?" He straightened the cuffs of his shirt while speaking.

"And if I'd moved to a new practice?"

"Their assessment of you suggested that that was never really an option, but that's why there are several chosen ones. We're all vets."

"But you only joined the practice a few months ago?"

"Uh-huh."

"So, who was watching over me before then?" I asked sarcastically. What was I thinking? Why was I having this discussion with Matthew? Why did anything he say matter? Other than the fact that it was so disconcerting. One half of my brain knew that Matthew had kidnapped me, that he was part of an organisation that wanted to open a portal into Hell. But it was Matthew! The vet that everyone loved. I just couldn't reconcile what Matthew had done with what I knew about him. He was charming and witty, caring and kind. Had it all been an act?

"Suffice it to say that we've had eyes on you."

"Who? Tell me… who?" I demanded, thinking that I'd never be able to trust anyone ever again unless I knew who else had been watching me… assuming I survived the next few days, that is.

"That's above my pay grade, Emma," Matthew replied, making it very clear that he could not be moved on this. "Now then, please have something to eat and drink, and then you might as well have a shower. You've been in those clothes for far too long."

Matthew was proving to be an enigma. In some ways, he seemed to care about my well-being, but he'd faked a breakdown in order to kidnap me. He'd clearly planned what he'd done because he'd been prepared for it, but he was apologetic about having drugged me. He was obviously part of an organisation that harboured ill-intent, but he was doing his utmost to distance himself from it. He'd never once said 'we,' only ever 'they.' Did he hold a grudge against his family? Or did he hold a grudge against me? He had said that his life had been dictated by mine after all. I think I'd be a bit peeved if my family had forced me to live my life a certain way just because that's how someone else chose to live theirs.

"Please," Matthew interrupted my musings.

"Fine," I huffed, reaching for a bottle of water and a sandwich from the pile of foodstuffs on the table. I didn't want to be too close to Matthew though, so I snatched what I wanted and retreated to the bed. I didn't even check what was in the sandwich.

"You can sit with me if you want. I don't bite."

"No, but you do drug unsuspecting colleagues."

"That was a one-time thing."

"Forgive me if I don't believe you," I bit back before unscrewing the cap from the bottle of water and finally having a drink. A chorus of angels sang in delight. The water was pleasantly cool, not so cold as to give me brain freeze but not too warm either. "You can go," I added, looking over at Matthew.

"I thought you might like some company." Matthew looked crestfallen.

"I don't. I don't like to associate with people like you."

Matthew's expression changed in an instant. He stood, pulled his shirt cuffs straight (again!), smoothed out his tie, and buttoned his jacket together. "There are toiletries in the bag there." He glanced down at the floor where there was indeed a washbag as well as some more bottles of water. "I suggest you use them," he snapped before crossing the room, yanking open the door that had been locked earlier, and slamming it behind him as he left. I clearly heard a key turn in the lock and at least two bolts being slid into place. And then I was alone again.

In spite of what Matthew had said, I did try to escape. After wallowing in misery for a while of course. Once he'd gone, walking out of the room in a huff as though I was the one who'd kidnapped him and not vice versa, I'd flung myself on the bed and cried until my eyes were sore and there were no more tears left inside of me. Eventually I'd realised that I had two choices: I could either hop into the abyss, or I could get off my backside and actually do something about my situation.

First of all, I'd peed again, because well… you know! And then I'd rattled the door handle, hoping that, even though I'd heard Matthew lock the door, it would somehow magically open. It didn't, and I'd tugged as hard as I could. After that, I'd scoured the room for something that I could smash the window with. The heaviest object that wasn't bolted down was the remote control. It was as light as a feather, but I'd still thrown it at the window. It had bounced harmlessly off the glass, landing unscathed on the carpet.

Frustrated, I'd plonked myself back on the bed and had begun picking at the sandwich I'd chosen earlier on. The aftereffects of whatever drugs I'd been given were wearing off because I was finally starting to feel human again and there was no escaping the fact that I was getting hungry. Matthew had been right about one thing—starving myself to death really wasn't an option. If the choice was between saving mankind or my stomach, then my stomach was always going to win the war. And I didn't see how I could kill myself either. Only a couple of days ago I'd confidently declared to Ellie that I'd rather take my own life than let anyone use me to get to Blake, but now that that seemed to be my only choice, I found that I wanted to live.

The sandwich wasn't anything to write home about, it was egg mayonnaise on a plain brown roll, but it brought to mind memories of childhood picnics. How many times had Mum and Dad taken me and Scott (and Ellie of course!) to the beach with a cooler box full of egg mayonnaise butties wrapped in tin foil? Usually, the cooler box had also contained bottles of pop, ready-salted crisps, and a packet of chocolate biscuits. We'd spent hours chasing each other around, playing tag or football, before collapsing on a tartan rug that Mum had laid out on the sand. And then we'd eaten until our bellies were on the point of bursting.

Reminiscing about more innocent times brought on a fresh set of the waterworks. And I thought I'd cried the river dry! I didn't sob like I had done earlier though, I just sat morosely on the edge of the bed, nibbling on my sandwich while tears rolled unchecked down my cheeks. My thoughts wandered aimlessly about: what would happen to Cooper and Watson when I was dead? Because I was going to die, wasn't I? I couldn't even find a way out of the room; I certainly wasn't going to be able to hold my own against a horde of demons. And it was all well and good for Johnna to say that I had to have faith and trust in Ellie, but Ellie didn't even know where I was. *I* didn't even know where I was.

I pulled my mind back to Cooper and Watson and pictured their sweet faces, sending a quick prayer to anyone who might be listening (despite being a non-believer) that someone would feed them when they realised I was missing. A smile ghosted my face. They'd be missing me. Well, that wasn't quite true; they'd be missing the sweeties that I gave them on a regular basis just because they were so darn cute! Maybe my mum and dad would take them in? Although it would be better if Ellie had them, but Ellie lived in an apartment now and that wasn't really an option. Cooper and Watson were used to having their own garden after all.

I did my utmost not to think about Blake because my heart was already hurting at the prospect of what we'd both face in the near future, but eventually his face rose unbidden in my mind's eye. Where was he? Why hadn't he answered me earlier on? Was he being held captive somewhere? I mean, I assumed not because well, you know, he was incorporeal to all but me but... maybe the demons had found a way? That had to be it because if that wasn't it, why hadn't I been able to pull him to me? Briefly my insecurities grabbed hold and told me that perhaps Blake didn't want me anymore, but A: even if that was true, I should still have been able to pull him to me; and B: in my heart of hearts, I didn't believe that was the case. Blake and I loved each other. I'd finally said those infamous words, I'd finally accepted it, and in the last few days, we'd been more settled somehow.

When my sandwich was all gone, I stood to toss the wrapper in the bin and, while on my feet, decided that I might as well have a shower. Matthew had been right about one thing: I'd been in my clothes for far too long, and while I didn't want to impress anyone (or get into the habit of obeying Matthew), there was no denying that I was starting to smell.

The shower was really only a hose that had been connected to the taps in the bath, but the water was hot, so I took the time to wash my hair and scrub myself all over with the toiletries that Matthew had left. I didn't linger; I didn't want Matthew (or anyone else for that matter) barging in on me while I was standing there naked and soapy. But, and I hated to admit it, by the time I was done, I did feel better.

I couldn't have been more than ten minutes in the shower, but when I'd finished, the bathroom had filled with steam—that's how hot the water had been. Hoping that my ancestors had some advice for me, I quickly towelled myself dry, dressed in the clothes that had been left, only because I wanted out of my work uniform, and stared into the mirror.

"Johnna?" I whispered, hoping that she'd appear. She didn't, but my nan did.

Remember to use the power of your ancestors when the time is right, she said, her face obscured by condensation.

A feeling of relief washed over me. I wasn't alone, not completely anyway. "Johnna said that it was all on Ellie now."

You'll need us too.

I nodded, not really understanding. "I'm going to die, aren't I?"

I sniffed, unconsciously rubbing my eyes.

The prophecy can be read in two ways, child. Have faith in your friend, and be ready when the time comes, my nan finished, slowly disappearing from sight.

Chapter 10 – Blake
Sunday 2nd June 2019

Blake had left Ellie's apartment, needing to escape. Abaddon had filled the space in a way that no mere mortal could, and she'd been annoying Blake, joking about everything and nothing. In the end, Ellie had suggested he leave, promising that she'd update him as soon as possible. Blake hadn't even thought about how she'd update him, he'd simply vanished, eventually finding himself at the North Pole.

He'd gone to an American casino first, hoping to lose himself in the eternal gloom of the place. People had been wandering about, not taking any notice of him. Usually he loved being in among such a crowd—he found that he could lose himself, almost pretend that he was 'real,' just like everyone else. But the crowd had irritated him; there were too many people enjoying themselves, having fun, laughing. It wasn't right, not when Emma was missing.

He'd moved on to the favelas of Rio de Janeiro, where he'd wandered through the narrow alleyways of Rocinha as people pushed past each other, hurrying on their way to somewhere else. The hustle and bustle of the city that resided within the beating heart of Rio itself had a comforting hum. The tiny dwellings, each filled with a family that knew no other way of living, pulsed with life. But Blake didn't want to be reminded of how good life could be.

Translocating again, he'd found himself in Tanzania, in the Ngorongoro Crater. He'd thought that by being where there were fewer people, where nature ruled, he'd finally be able to think and find a degree of solace. Zebra and antelope had roamed the grasslands all around him; flamingos had crowded together, standing at the edge of a lake that stretched away into the distance; and a solitary leopard had lapped at the water from the shoreline. The leopard had been Blake's undoing, because of Emma's love of cats.

He'd left Ngorongoro Crater and found himself at the North Pole, standing on one of the ice caps that floated lazily on the surface of the Arctic Ocean. No matter which way he turned, the landscape was pure white. From one horizon to the other, all he could see were huge snow drifts, piled into mounds by the wind and frozen solid by the freezing temperatures that plummeted every night. Overhead, the sun shone weakly from a brilliant bright blue sky. The place was deserted and tranquil.

Blake crumpled to the ground in a heap and sobbed, his heart broken in two. Emma was missing. He knew that she wasn't dead because he hadn't needed to reap her soul, but knowing that didn't give him any comfort. She was missing and he couldn't find her. He couldn't even help Abaddon search for her, let alone do something practical like ring the police. All he could do was wait. Why hadn't she pulled him to her? Didn't she want him anymore? Had he complained once too often? A kernel of guilt started to grow inside him, swelling to epic proportions. He hadn't believed her when she'd said she was being haunted, and now he hadn't done enough to protect her. If something happened to her, it would be his fault. He desperately wanted to wrap his arms around her, to tell her that he loved her, that he was sorry for everything he'd done wrong, for all the times that he'd been indifferent to her plight, for all the times that he'd complained about her ability to control him.

Blake cried for a long time. Tears ran down his cheeks and dripped from his chin only to disappear into the ether, and while he cried, something shifted within him. He'd spent centuries thinking only of himself. He'd been so wrapped up in his own suffering that he'd failed to feel any compassion for others. He'd been oblivious to the anguish of loss. He'd been unable to comprehend the agony of pain. And he'd had no sympathy for those on their deathbeds. Such things had been nothing more than a part of life to him. Now, though, he had some understanding of those things, and it shook him to his core.

Eventually Blake's tears ran dry, but he didn't move. He had no need to because he was impervious to the cold. He couldn't feel the chill emanating from the ground, nor could he feel the bitter wind stinging his face.

As he lay quietly on the ground, he started to turn things over in his mind. He'd learned so much recently, but there were things that remained a mystery. He now knew how he'd come into being, and he knew about the three dimensions, about angels and demons. But he didn't know why he'd never seen any until Abaddon. Could they hide what they were? He knew that Ellie, and each guardian who'd lived before her, had active angel blood in their veins, that they'd been given it to help them guard the Key, that they'd been told of his existence so that they were prepared to stop the Key—to stop Emma—from being used to force him to open a portal into the other dimensions. But he didn't know how each one in turn had kept their memories from him when he'd reaped their souls. Did the angel blood interfere with his abilities somehow?

With a sigh, Blake sat up to find Seith watching over him, waiting patiently.

"Seith." Blake glanced upwards, making eye contact. "What do you mean, 'it's a start'?" he asked in response to Seith's unspoken statement, but before Seith could answer, Abaddon appeared, and the peace and quiet of the North Pole was immediately shattered.

"Jesus Christ, Blake, you can go anywhere. Literally anywhere. Why in God's name would you choose here?"

"Have you found her?" Blake asked, ignoring Abaddon's comment, rising to his feet.

"It's bloody freezing here. Look what I've had to wear just to keep warm." Abaddon gestured towards her clothing. She'd chosen the body of a native and had on their traditional garb: sealskin kamiks with duffle sock liners, a caribou parka that had an inner woollen jacket, and a knitted cap underneath the fur-lined hood of her coat. The only bare skin that Blake could see were her rosy red cheeks and her violet eyes.

"Have. You. Found. Her?" Blake asked again.

"Seriously. Is that all you're going to ask? Nothing about how I might be?"

Blake didn't answer, choosing instead to glare at Abaddon.

"Fine," she huffed in reply, rolling her eyes. "I might have done," she concluded before winking mischievously and saying, "I'll race you back to Ellie's." And with that, she was gone.

Chapter 11 – Ellie
Sunday 2nd June 2019

"What on earth possessed him to go to the bloody North Pole?" Abaddon muttered as she landed back in Ellie's apartment. Turning in a circle, she quickly changed her look, choosing to appear as Ellie's identical twin, even going so far as to match her clothing.

"What do you mean, 'the North Pole'?" Ellie asked. "And you're not staying like that."

"Why not?" Abaddon argued. "Don't you think I look pretty?" She smiled coyly at Ellie.

Ellie blushed. How could she answer that question without coming across as conceited? "Well, yes, but…" she started to say. Damn Abaddon's peculiar powers.

"Scott." Abaddon looked over to where he was sitting on the sofa. "What do you think?" Without giving Scott time to answer her, she giggled, caught hold of Ellie, twirled her in a circle, and then went to sit on Scott's knee. Scott had already pulled Abaddon into him when the real Ellie gave the game away.

"Scott!" She dragged Abaddon off his knee.

"Spoilsport," Abaddon declared.

Scott, who was clearly confused by Abaddon's antics, asked, "What? I thought it was you. Wait! Who's who?" It seemed impossible for him to tell one from the other.

"Abaddon, stop it!" Ellie glared at Abaddon, who glared right back at Ellie with exactly the same glint in her eye.

"Ellie's on the left. Abaddon's on the right. Now, where's Emma?" Blake announced, interrupting the conversation.

"How can you tell?" Abaddon asked, a puzzled look creasing her brow.

"How can you tell what?" Scott interjected, twisting around in his seat, seemingly baffled by the sudden turn in the conversation.

"It's Blake, he's here, and he can tell us apart," Ellie absently answered Scott, the scowl fading from her face as a new idea bubbled up from the back of her mind. "Abaddon," she asked, "can you do something to Scott so that he can see Blake? Can you do what you did to me?"

"I can, but it's going to hurt, and it will only be temporary," Abaddon answered.

"It didn't hurt me. Well, that bit didn't anyway."

"No, because you have angel blood in your veins. Your body was primed. Scott's is not. It will hurt." Abaddon took on the mannerisms of a schoolteacher who was explaining something for the umpteenth time.

"How much will it hurt?" Ellie asked, ignoring Abaddon's sarcastic jibe. "Scott needs to be able to see Blake. And how temporary is temporary?"

"It will really hurt, but it will last for long enough."

"And will you do it?" Ellie asked, despite the fact that Scott was trying to interrupt.

"I will, but only if Blake explains how he could tell us apart," Abaddon answered. "And how did you know it was me at the North Pole?" She looked over at Blake.

"Don't I get a say?" Scott asked while Blake answered Abaddon's question.

"Who else would it have been at the North Pole?"

"And now?" Abaddon persisted.

"Ellie's eyes are clouded with worry. Yours are not."

"You can see that?" Abaddon frowned.

"I've spent a lot of time watching people. I notice things. Now, where's Emma?"

"I only said that I might have found her," Abaddon started, "but before I tell you anything, I do agree with Ellie. Scott needs to be in on the act."

"I want to know where Emma is." Blake spoke through gritted teeth.

"All in good time, Blakey, all in good time," Abaddon declared, taking a step towards Scott, lifting the palm of her hand up towards her mouth and blowing something in Scott's face.

"Wait—" Scott started to say, but it was too late. His breathing quickly became laboured, and he turned scarlet. Leaning forward, he rested his elbows on his knees and cradled his head in his hands, moaning quietly to himself.

"Abaddon!" Ellie exclaimed, darting to the sofa to sit beside Scott.

"What?" Abaddon shrugged nonchalantly. "I told you it would hurt. It's only meant to be used on people like you. I'm told that it feels like a swarm of ants is tunnelling their way inside of your body, biting off chunks of your flesh as they go."

"You could have warned me it was going to be that bad," Ellie snapped.

"Pfft!" Abaddon pooh-poohed, absently inspecting her nails. "That would have only made it worse. Anyway," she stepped forward and grabbed hold of Scott's chin, forcing him to look up at her, "it looks like it's settling down now."

Scott opened his eyes and jerked his head to one side, freeing himself from Abaddon's hold. "Ow!" He scowled at Abaddon.

"Has it worked?" Ellie asked, rubbing Scott's arm gently. "Can you see Abaddon for who she really is?"

"I think so. I mean, yeah, I guess so. Is this what it's like for you?" Scott replied, glancing quickly at Ellie before turning back to stare at Abaddon some more.

"What can you see?"

"Abaddon. I can see Abaddon. Well, I assume it's Abaddon," Scott said, shrugging his shoulders. "But I can also see you... it's weird."

"That's what it's like for me as well. I can see who Abaddon presents herself as, but I can also see her as an angel. The image sort of flickers."

"Yeah..." Scott nodded. "And just for the record," he turned so that he could focus all of his attention on Ellie, "I was going to ask what it would feel like so that I could better prepare myself. No matter how much I love you, you don't get to make my decisions for me."

Ellie had the good grace to look contrite. She glanced down before apologising. "I'm sorry, you're right, I should have asked. I just need this to be over. I need to find Emma almost as much as Blake does." Her voice trembled with emotion.

"I know. I do too," Scott replied softly. "It's a good job you're so cute." He leaned over and kissed her chastely on the lips before standing and facing Blake. "Blake," he acknowledged before muttering to himself, "this is so bloody weird."

"Where. Is. Emma?" Blake almost exploded with rage.

"Blake!" Ellie gasped, shocked by his sudden outburst.

"Are you not worried?" Blake spat the words.

"Of course I'm worried. We're all worried, but Scott needed to be able to see you if we're going to work together." Ellie stood and stepped closer to Blake to offer him a degree of comfort, but Blake backed out of reach.

"Incorporeal being, remember?"

"Of course, I just... we're all frightened, Blake. For Emma and because of what might happen."

"Actually," Abaddon interrupted, "I'm not frightened. I miss the good old days when angels and demons used this world as a battleground."

"Abaddon," Ellie narrowed her eyes, "now is not the time. And, please, will you change your look?"

"Fine," Abaddon muttered and shook her head. In doing so, she changed the colour of her hair, from Ellie's natural blonde to a bright cobalt colour. That was all that she changed though. She turned to glance at her reflection in one of the big picture windows and smiled. "I like it! Have you ever thought about going blue?"

Ellie didn't answer; she just glared at Abaddon.

"What?" Abaddon asked as if all she'd done was suggest that Ellie might pass her a pen. "You really do need to lighten up. I mean, come on, your body is banging. You should be out there making the most of it while you're young enough to enjoy it, before you tie yourself to one man... to him." She cocked her head at Scott. "Maybe try on some hot pants once in a while. Or how about—"

"Ellie is perfect just the way she is, thank you very much," Scott interrupted.

"His soulmate is missing," Ellie announced, pointing at Blake before turning to point at Scott. "His sister is missing," she added. She spoke quietly but definitely. "And my best friend is missing. Now is not the time for your antics." There was no denying that Abaddon was good fun, but given how serious things were, Ellie's temper was starting to fray. Although at least she still had a tight grip on it. If the roles had been reversed and she'd been the one missing, Emma would have lost hers already.

"You make it sound like three different people are missing, not just one."

"Abaddon!" Ellie snapped. "Can we please get on with it? Now that Scott can *see*, we really should be making a plan. The police won't have any luck finding Emma; we're her only chance."

"For goodness sake." Abaddon rolled her eyes. "Okay, gather round, children," she continued, indicating that Ellie, Scott, and Blake should sit together on the sofa.

Ellie and Scott were quick to do as instructed, but Blake remained standing, his body tense and his face stern.

"Blakey," Abaddon whined, clenching her fists together and stamping one of her feet. "Come and sit with the others. You're ruining everything."

"No," Blake answered.

"But Blaaakeeey…"

"No. Enough's enough."

"Fine." Abaddon crossed her arms, pouting. "But you're taking all of the fun out of this."

"Fun?" Blake spat. "Emma's life is at stake; this isn't a game."

"Blake—" Ellie started to say but was cut off by Abaddon.

"Ha! You think Emma's life is the only one at stake. Demons could very well escape from Hell in only four days' time. We could be overrun by the buggers soon, and all you care about is your precious little Emma. Never mind Emma, all of humanity is at risk. And you'll all remember," she gestured around the room, "that I was the only one in favour of ending her life to stop this situation from occurring. If we'd done that when we had the chance—"

"We were never going to do that, Abaddon," Ellie interrupted. "And even if we had, Emma's soul would have been reborn. What would you have had us do? Murder every child born with the soul for all of eternity?"

"Well, no," Abaddon answered, her face softening for a moment. "But anyway," she continued with a sniff, "it's too late now. Now we have to put our lives on the line in order to mount a rescue attempt."

"Your life isn't really on the line though, is it?" Scott asked.

"I'll have you know, I might have lived for longer than you, I might be able to do more than you, but I'm not immortal. I'm not him." Abaddon pointed at Blake.

"I apologise." Scott held his hands up in mock surrender. "I just assumed that angels couldn't be killed."

"Don't be ridiculous," Abaddon replied, a little tartly. "Of course angels can be killed, and it's a good job too. Angels and demons are opposite ends of the spectrum; if angels can't be killed, demons can't be killed either, and if you're going to stop what's coming, you'll going to need to be able to kill demons."

"Oh." Scott's face flushed bright red.

Abaddon glanced around the room before muttering, "I accept your apology. And now, I suppose we'd better get on with it. Time is of the essence after all." The accusatory tone of her voice left Ellie in no doubt that Abaddon blamed everyone but herself for the delays, but she held her tongue. "Right, what do you lot actually know about angels and demons?" she asked.

"Nothing really," Ellie answered. "Only what you've told me previously. Angels are good—"

"Ha," Scott muttered quietly beside Ellie.

"—and demons are bad," Ellie continued, ignoring Scott's interruption. "You guys used to fight all the time."

"We did!" Abaddon smiled, her face lighting up. "Oh! The battles we used to have. You should have seen me in my battle gear. Wait! Let me show you…" Abaddon spun in a quick circle, changing her entire look. By the time she was facing forwards again, all signs of Ellie had disappeared. Instead, Abaddon the angel had appeared in all her seven-foot-tall glory. She wasn't even wearing heels; her shoes were nothing more than a leather sole with thongs that crisscrossed over her feet before wrapping around her ankles.

"Woah!" Scott exclaimed. Abaddon was slim and muscular with long white-blonde hair that had been pulled into a high ponytail and threaded through the top of a golden-coloured helmet. Her body armour, which matched her helmet in design, encased her chest and abdomen but left much of her back bare so that her pearlescent wings could move freely. Her arms and legs were also bare, but she did have on something that looked like a skirt, apart from the fact that it had metal blades hanging down from the waist, showing only hints of white fabric underneath.

"I know," Abaddon purred, evidentially delighted with Scott's response. "I look gorgeous, don't I? When me and the Destroyer took to the field—"

"The Destroyer?" Scott asked, a quizzical look crossing his face.

"My blade," Abaddon explained, seemingly unfazed by the interruption. "When we took to the field, demons quailed in their boots. Many simply threw down their weapons and fled in fear, such was my reputation."

"I thought *you* were The Destroyer?" Scott asked.

"Me?"

"Yes, I've been reading about you on the internet, ever since I first found out about you."

"Pfft." Abaddon pulled a face, dismissing Scott with a wave of her hand. "Anyway, before Blake has a coronary..." she continued, glancing in his direction. He'd not moved a muscle, and his face was still clouded with anger. "Where were we? Ah yes! Angels and demons are opposite ends of the spectrum; they're organised differently. Angels don't bother with any kind of structure. We don't feel the need. We work together when we need to, but otherwise we go off and do our own thing. We don't worry about keeping an eye on each other because we trust that no one is going to do anything... well, anything silly. Demons, on the other hand, don't trust each other. They're organised into hierarchical families, and they're constantly at war with one another. Even within a family, there's in-fighting. They don't always get on, you see. That's how I was able to get a hint of where Emma might be."

"And where's that?" Blake asked, his voice thick with emotion.

"I'm getting to that." Abaddon huffed. "There are several demon families in the U.K., but one is more active than the others, the Demiurges. They've been here for centuries, and they've always been obsessed with reopening the portal. Half of their family was in Hell when John did what he did and well... you know." She waved a hand in Blake's general direction. "They're desperate to be reunited with their brethren. With good reason, they would argue. When the whole family is together, they're a force to be reckoned with. They'd undoubtedly be the 'top dog,' if only they were all top side..." She paused and laughed. "Do ya see what I did there? No?" She shook her head before muttering, "Honestly, I need a better audience."

"Abaddon," Ellie pleaded, wanting to get Abaddon back on track.

"The problem with the Demiurges," Abaddon continued,

ignoring the interruption, "is that they're minted. Like, beyond minted. They're richer than God himself, and He could create money out of thin air if He really wanted to. They have their fingers in so many pies that it wasn't enough just to suspect that they were the ones who'd nabbed Emma. I needed to be certain, and I needed to know which branch of the family was in the lead. So, I, erm… weeell… I kind of got chummy with a demon." A flush brightened Abaddon's cheeks. "And just for the record, the rescue mission is a favour, but I had to spend fifty quid to get Davril to open up. I expect that money back."

"You want me to reimburse you? For what?" Ellie exclaimed.

Abaddon looked offended. "For the drinks I had to buy Davril. I certainly wasn't going to sleep with him! I do have some standards, you know, but what I don't have is the wealth of the Demiurges behind me."

Ellie frowned. "You had drinks with a demon?"

"Yes, how else was I going to find out where Emma's being held?"

"I don't know. I assumed you kept track of demon hideouts."

"Why on God's green Earth would I do that? I've got much better things to do with my time."

"But… you're enemies. You used to slaughter each other on the battlefield."

Abaddon tittered. "I know. Those were the good old days. But we've been trapped here for a long time; some of us have learned to be civil with each other."

"Ooh-kay." Ellie continued to lead the conversation. "So, what did this Davril have to say?"

"Well…" Abaddon started, putting an inordinate amount of emphasis on the word, "he didn't say all that much, but he did say that his brother was the biggest of all dickheads."

"And that helps us how?"

"Don't you see?"

Ellie and Scott shook their heads. Blake didn't move.

"Davril and his twin never fall out… like ever. They must be in on what's happening or else they wouldn't have had any reason to argue."

"Abaddon," Ellie pulled a face, "that's the most tenuous link I've ever heard in all my life."

Abaddon crossed her arms over her body. "We don't have

anything else to go on, do we? I mean, Davril did mutter something about 'that bloody Emma,' but he clammed up at that point. I couldn't get anything else out of him, and I couldn't exactly torture him, could I? I mean, I guess I could have followed him when he left, but I figured I had enough to go on, and we do try to avoid bloodshed nowadays. It's a bit difficult to explain away the colour of our blood."

"For God's sake, Abaddon," Ellie was almost in tears. "Where's Emma?"

"Oh, yes, that. Well, I don't know exactly where she is—"

"Abaddon," Blake said quietly, the menacing tone of his voice leaving Ellie in no doubt that he was a pressure kettle about to explode.

"Oh calm down, Blakey. I was going to say that I don't know exactly where she is, but assuming Davril and his twin are involved, then Emma must be being held in one of the houses that they own. There are only three in the U.K. We'll need to check each of them out in turn." She smiled brightly, almost as though she'd just handed out the answer to lasting world peace.

"And where are they?"

"Before I tell you anything else, I want you all," Abaddon glanced around the whole room, looking Ellie, Scott, and Blake in the eye, "to promise me that you won't do anything rash." She paused, waiting for an answer. When none was forthcoming, she crossed her arms together, tilted her chin downwards, and arched one of her eyebrows.

"Fine, I promise," Ellie replied, feeling like a school child.

"Me too," Scott added.

Abaddon smiled at them both and then looked over to Blake. He didn't answer, but he did incline his head briefly.

"Well then…" Abaddon twitched a wing and one of the picture windows was immediately replaced with a map, complete with three red dots, each labelled precisely with full coordinates. One of the red dots was in central London; one of them appeared to be in the middle of nowhere, somewhere in Scotland; and the third was on the outskirts of Chester.

Blake glanced only briefly at the map before disappearing.

"Oh, for f—"

"Abaddon!" Ellie interjected sharply. "What…?"

"Bloody hell! Now, I'm going to have to go and rescue him

before we can start rescuing Emma," Abaddon ranted. Ellie and Scott turned quickly in their seats, realising what had happened: Blake had gone to search for Emma himself. "He promised he wouldn't do anything rash," Abaddon continued. "And do you know why I made him promise that?" She didn't wait for an answer. "Well, I'll tell you why, because they'll have the place covered in runes. He could very well be walking into a trap. You two," she barked, "hit the net and do some research on the three locations. I'll be back with him in a jiffy," she finished, and then vanished, leaving Ellie and Scott looking at each other open-mouthed.

Chapter 12 – Blake
Sunday 2nd June 2019

    Blake was standing on a side road in London, one that was lined with evenly spaced trees and neatly parked cars giving it the quiet, secluded feel of a suburb. Blake didn't care about either the trees or the cars; he was staring at a large, detached house set back from the road. It had stone steps leading up to a dark red front door, and it was the first of the locations that Abaddon had shown him. It took only a thought and Blake was inside.

    The hallway was narrower than Blake had been expecting. Immediately in front of him, on the right, was a set of stairs leading up to the first floor, and around a corner, he found the formal living room and a big open-plan kitchen-diner. From the silence, it was apparent that no one lived there. In fact, the house appeared to have been packed away. The fridge-freezer had been unplugged; the cupboards were bare; and upstairs, the wardrobes were empty.

    Blake still took the time to walk through all three floors, not that he found anything of interest, and certainly nothing that indicated Emma had ever been held hostage there. Satisfied, he translocated to the second location that Abaddon had shown him.

    It appeared to be colder in Scotland than it had been in London. In London, the trees had been lush and green, but here, north of the Cairngorms, summer had barely awoken. Plant life was only just coming into bud.

    The castle—because that was the only word that could be used to describe the building in front of Blake—appeared to be deserted, just like the house in London had been, but Blake had to be sure. This time, he climbed the stone steps up to the front door, which was the same dark red as the one in London, but the one in London had been painted to give it a glossy finish, this one had been stained. It was more in keeping with the stonework of the building.

    Blake crossed the threshold without any problems but found only empty rooms, all of which were decorated in much the same way:

beige with accents of dark red. Frustrated not to have found Emma yet, Blake clenched his fists tightly together and bellowed out his rage before moving on for the third time. His temper was starting to rise. Panic was threatening to tear apart his sanity. Why hadn't he found her? How could he save her if he couldn't even find her? Perhaps Abaddon had been lying to him? Perhaps she'd sent him on a wild goose chase? Though she had tried to extract a promise from him that he wouldn't do anything rash, so perhaps not. Rash? How could he do anything rash, bound as he was by unseen chains, given only the power to reap the souls of man?

Almost immediately Blake knew that there was something different about the last property. For starters, it was massive. The house in London had been big, the castle in Scotland had been… well, a castle, but neither had come close to what Blake found in Chester. Not only that, but there were several parked cars scattered about on the circular driveway, suggesting that this house was lived in. The panic that had taken hold of Blake abated somewhat, replaced with a tiny flicker of hope.

The house in Chester—or more accurately the mansion—sat a good way back from the road behind a red brick wall that was topped with iron railings. It had a Georgian look about it. Marble columns supported a large porchway, and in the centre of the porchway there was a set of dark red double doors. The windows on both the upper and lower floors were all neatly aligned and evenly spaced. The grounds were perfectly manicured.

There was no denying that the house was beautiful, but a peculiar buzz emanated from it. It wasn't exactly a buzz. It was more like a hum, but it wasn't quite that either. Blake couldn't hear anything, but the air around him vibrated. The pressure that it created was a novel sensation, not least because he'd never been able to feel anything without Emma by his side.

Remembering Abaddon's plea not to do anything rash and because of the peculiar sensation that came off the house, Blake decided to walk the perimeter before doing anything else. The buzzing-hum forced him to keep his distance and while he grew increasingly desperate to search the building, every time he thought about translocating inside, the pressure became too great, and he found himself backing off. Blake had walked for a while before something forced him to a standstill. The tiny flicker of hope that he'd felt only moments before was snuffed out by an unexpected wave of despair that came crashing down on him. He was drowning, and only Emma could save him.

"Emma!" Blake shouted out loud, hoping that by some miracle she could hear him. Using the strength of his love for her, he was able to take a step closer to the building despite the feeling of pressure. A wisp of emotion danced across his skin in response to his cry. "Emma." Blake breathed a sigh of relief.

"Blake! Stop!" Abaddon shouted from behind him.

Blake spun to face her, surprised that he'd not heard her approach.

"You!" He felt no guilt about deceiving Abaddon. He'd made no promises, not in the same way that Ellie and Scott had anyway. And no one was going to keep him from finding Emma, least of all Abaddon.

"Were you expecting someone else?" Abaddon asked mildly, but the sneer on her face told Blake that she was not amused.

"You shouldn't have followed me."

"Well, it's a good job I did because now that I've saved your sorry ass, you owe me one."

"You haven't saved me from anything. I'm immortal, remember? You said so yourself."

"Oh wise one," Abaddon mocked. "If only all you had to worry about was your life."

Blake raised an eyebrow before turning away to take another step closer to the building.

"Fine! Go ahead and trap yourself in a snare. See if I care," Abaddon muttered, just loud enough for Blake to hear.

Blake stilled and turned back to Abaddon. "A snare?"

"Yes, Blake, a snare. But you keep doing what you're doing."

Indecision creased Blake's brow. He wanted to ignore Abaddon. His loathing for her was unparalleled, but for some reason, he believed her. Maybe her abilities affected him along with everyone else. "What's a snare?" he asked eventually.

"A snare? Oh, pfft," Abaddon waved her hand dismissively, "it's nothing. It will only trap you for all of eternity."

"That's not possible."

"Isn't it?" Abaddon cocked her head to one side. "Not that long ago, you didn't even know angels and demons existed, and now you're an expert on what's possible and what's not?"

"But…" Blake started to say before words failed him. Abaddon had known exactly how to undermine Blake's self-confidence. "Why—?"

"Why hasn't anyone used it on you before now?" Abaddon interrupted. "Or would you prefer to know why you didn't know about it in the first place? There's a lot that you don't know about angels and demons, Blake. We've known about you, but you've not known about us. We've always been able to see you, to hear you. We could have talked to you whenever we wanted to, but we didn't. We didn't want to. You were no use to us until you met the Key, and that's why no one's bothered to set a trap for you before now. We left you alone because we didn't need you." The tone of Abaddon's words made it clear that she was being purposely hurtful.

"Why are you helping me then?" Blake's voice was thick with emotion.

"To be entirely honest with you, I'm not exactly sure. God charged me with creating and caring for the line of guardians. I've done that. I don't need to do anything else, but here we are." Abaddon shrugged, before continuing, "I've always thought that the plan was to kill the first Key who came into contact with you, but that won't solve the problem that John created. The soul will only be reborn."

"That still doesn't explain why you're helping me."

"Ellie believes in Emma. That's why I'm helping you."

Blake didn't bother to ask Abaddon to elaborate further even though he didn't understand her answer. Instead, he called for Seith, and when Seith appeared, he pointed behind him. "She's in there, I can feel her love for me." He stared hard at Abaddon before turning to face Seith. "Stand guard, but don't go in. Abaddon said something about a snare. I'll go and fill Ellie and Scott in."

It was Abaddon's turn to look puzzled. "The place is warded. Your connection to her has been cut."

"Evidently, neither the angels nor the demons know everything there is to know about Emma and I then, do they?" Blake replied, a slight smile turning up the corners of his mouth before he disappeared. At the very least, his budding hope had not been completely washed away. He now knew where Emma was; he just didn't know how to help her.

Chapter 13 – Emma
Sunday 2nd June 2019

Boredom forced me to do it. I wasn't all that good at just sitting around, and after more than twenty-four hours with nothing to do, I couldn't stand it any longer. Yes, I'd been able to use the bathroom at will. Yes, I'd had access to a television. And yes, I'd been provided with enough junk food to keep myself on a sugar high for weeks, but goddammit, I was bored. I'd cried, I'd slept, I'd worked myself up into a fury, I'd slept some more, I'd stared out of the window—there wasn't anything to see, mind you. I'd even done some exercises: only a few star jumps and some squats, but that had been enough to remind me that I didn't really do exercise. I could spend all day out in the garden, happily weeding and hoeing, but actual exercise... urgh!

"Matthew!" I hollered, hammering on the locked door, although I was doing my utmost not to think about the fact that it was locked. Thinking about that would only remind me that I was being held against my will, which would bring on a fresh set of the waterworks. No, I wasn't going to think about any of that; instead, I was hanging on to the last thing that my nan had said to me in the mirror. She'd said that I had to have faith, and I was taking that to mean that there was still hope. As a consequence, I was doing my best ostrich impression: I was busy burying my head in the sand and ignoring the reality of my situation. "Matthew!" I banged on the door again. There was no answer. There'd been no answer for at least five minutes now, and I was starting to feel winded. In a huff, I turned around and leant against the door, only for it to open outwards. Naturally I fell to the floor with a bump. Grace and elegance had never been my best friends.

"Matthew!" I exclaimed, looking upwards.

"Yes?" Matthew replied, helping me to my feet.

"I've been banging on the door for a while now. I thought you weren't coming."

"I'm not your babysitter; I do have other things to do. Besides," Matthew paused and sniffed disdainfully, "you wanted me to leave you alone."

"I did. I do," I added quickly, "but I'm also bored, and I'd like to be allowed outside. I assume that can be arranged seeing as how T, whoever that is, insinuated that I'm an honoured guest in the note that was left for me." I smiled coyly, looking up at Matthew from underneath my eyelashes, fluttering them ever so slightly. I didn't know if he would be immune to my feminine wiles, what with him being in league with demons, but I figured it was worth a try. That look always worked on my dad.

"T is Terrance. He's my father. And he didn't insinuate anything of the sort. His note merely said that you might as well use the bathroom. They need you to be cleansed after all." Flattery did not appear to be working.

"Pleeeaaase, Matthew."

Matthew huffed loudly. I'd almost given up when he finally said, "I'll have to get it approved. Back in there while I check." He pointed inside the room that I was hoping to get out of.

Dutifully I returned to my bedroom, also known as my prison, and sat on the end of the bed, counting out the seconds until I heard the key turn in the lock again.

"Come on then." Matthew opened the door wider. "You'll be handcuffed to me the whole time, mind you."

"Fine." Excitement bubbled up inside of me. I was finally getting to go outside. Even the thought of being handcuffed to Matthew didn't scare me. It should have, I knew that really, but I was all scared out, for now at least. I knew that I wasn't going to like some of what was coming—the memory of Ellie's dream had popped into my head earlier on, and I hadn't been able to stop myself from wondering if it had been prophetic—but for now, something positive was happening. Well, in so much as I'd gotten something that I'd asked for. On any other day, a normal one, being able to go outside wouldn't even crack the top ten of things to be thankful for. Today, it was number one, and if I'd had pen and paper to write out a list, I'd have highlighted the word 'outside' by drawing little stars around it, such was my excitement.

After cuffing me, Matthew led me down a long corridor. The walls were the same beige as the walls in my room, and more of those strange symbols had been painted along the top of each one, forming a banner. And I thought stencilling had gone out in the '80s. At regular intervals there were what I assumed were cameras, but I ignored those. I couldn't exactly do anything about them, could I? At least there weren't any in my bedroom or in my bathroom, not that I'd seen anyway.

"Matthew?" I asked. "What do the symbols mean?" I pointed towards the ceiling with my free hand.

"They're runes."

"Runes?" I repeated, testing the word for myself. "You called them that before, but what do they mean?" Now that I was looking at them, one in particular had caught my eye. It was made up of three horizontal lines stacked neatly on top of each other. The lines were all the same length, but the middle one was a zig-zag, whereas the other two were straight. "I've seen that one before." I indicated the one that I recognised.

"Hmmm, have you now?" Matthew asked, ignoring my question.

"You know I have. You painted it on my front door, didn't you?" Where else could I have seen a rune before?

"Well, I didn't, no. But I can see how you would jump to that conclusion."

"You know who did though, don't you?"

"I do, yes."

"How could you let them slaughter an animal and use their blood like that? Whatever else you are, you're still a vet."

Matthew paused and looked at me, his brow furrowed. Because he'd stopped, I was forced too as well. "What makes you think they used the blood of an animal?"

"Danny said…" I started to say before the meaning behind Matthew's words filtered into my consciousness. "It wasn't animal blood?" My stomach muscles clenched tightly together.

"Human sacrifices are much more potent."

"You killed someone?"

"Again, I didn't, no."

"Matthew, that's…" My voice trailed off because I didn't know how to respond. Matthew seemed so unconcerned about the fact that he'd just admitted to knowing a murderer.

"Whatever you're going to say, you needn't bother. It was necessary. Every sacrifice is necessary. In this case, they needed to ward your house, to start the process of cleansing you. Besides which, as I understand it, the rune helped you as well as us. It turned your home into a sanctuary, forcing the spirit that was haunting you to remain outside."

"You know about that?"

"I know about everything in your life, Emma. All of the chosen ones get a daily briefing."

"You get a daily briefing… about me? What the hell, Matthew? Don't you hear yourself?" My infamous temper was making a resurgence.

"Every Key throughout history has been watched. It's just part of their process. Now, do you want to go outside, or don't you?"

Numbly I nodded my head, but honestly, I didn't know what I wanted anymore. I just wanted to go home. I wanted to nestle in bed with Blake, with Cooper and Watson at our feet. I wanted to share a bowl of popcorn with Ellie while we snuggled together underneath a quilt and watched a movie. I wanted to go to my mum and dad's house and bicker with Scott about everything and nothing. In short, I wanted my life back. I wanted to unhear the fact that someone prepared a daily briefing about me because I really *didn't* want to think about what that meant.

Matthew and I carried on walking down the corridor until we came to a central landing. Another corridor stretched away in front of us, and to the left there was a reading nook, complete with big picture windows and a window seat stuffed full of cushions, with bookcases built in underneath it. Among the books, I spied a framed photograph of a young man dressed in a military uniform.

"Who's that?" I asked, pointing to the picture.

Matthew didn't even look where I pointed. "That's my great-grandfather."

"Oh!" I couldn't keep the surprise out of my voice. Obviously I knew that Matthew had family, he'd just told me his father's name, but I hadn't expected any signs of sentimentality in this house. "What was his name?" I asked.

"Edward."

"And he was in the army?"

"In World War One."

"Didn't you get on with him?" I asked. Despite my situation, Matthew's behaviour was intriguing.

"Frankly, Emma, it's none of your business," Matthew replied, pulling me towards a flight of stairs to our right, "but honestly, I never met him. He was dead before I was born. I assume he was a mean old bastard like the rest of my family."

The stairwell was wider than most, but other than that, it was a fairly normal stairwell, except for the photographs of Blake that covered the wall.

"Blake!" I gasped, my feet suddenly rooted to the floor, Matthew's family forgotten.

Matthew stopped beside me, a smirk on his face. "I wondered what you'd think of their little homage to **him**."

"But...? What...? How...?"

"Oh come now, Emma. I know that you know **he** can be seen in photographs. I've even got a copy of the one that you had taken over Easter."

"But..." I was at a loss for words; knowing that Matthew had a copy of mine and Blake's first couple's shot didn't even register.

"I suppose what you reeeally want to know," Matthew drawled, "is how do *they* know **he** can be caught on camera. Well," Matthew paused and winked at me, "I'll let you in on a little secret: they found out quite by accident. It waaas..." Matthew paused again, clearly thinking about something, "maybe... a hundred years ago, I think."

"But... how do they even know where he'll be?"

"They don't." Matthew frowned faintly. "I mean, occasionally the demons catch sight of **him**, but no one, not even the demons, can track him. It appears as if **he** can go wherever **he** wants, whenever **he** wants."

"Then how..." I left my question hanging but waved in the general direction of the photographs.

"Dumb luck mostly, and a lot of money."

"I don't understand."

"Nowadays it's much easier of course. Everybody shares everything about their lives on social media. They take pictures of anything and everything, and it's all uploaded. All *they* had to do was hack into the internet, set up the search parameters, and voila."

"But—" I started to say.

"Oh Emma! You do say that a lot," Matthew interrupted. "Come, let me point out my favourites," he finished, tugging me further down the stairwell. "This one, right here," Matthew pointed at a black and white photograph in which Blake stood off-centre gazing into the distance, "is the oldest image. They didn't even know what they had at first. No, they'd collected the image for another reason, but one of the demons happened to see it and recognised **him** for who **he** was. It—"

"How's this even possible?" I butted in, still staring at the wall in front of me. There were hundreds of photographs and every single one of them featured Blake. In most of them, he was blurred. He was obviously not the focal point, and he wasn't always looking at the camera. More often than not, he was either staring off into the distance or else he was facing away from the camera, but it was definitely him. He was usually surrounded by people, part of a crowd but apart from it, and his face was devoid of emotion.

"Which one do you like best, Emma?" Matthew asked, not bothering to answer my question.

"I…" I didn't know what to say. I wasn't very often at a loss for words, but I was literally speechless.

"How about this one?" Matthew pulled me further down the stairwell and pointed to what was obviously a new addition. It showed Blake in full colour on a sunny day. A slight smile curled up the corners of his mouth, and his eyes sparkled brightly.

"He's beautiful," I whispered, reaching up to touch the glass in front of the image. I couldn't help myself.

"This was taken not so long ago, after **he'd** met you."

"I still don't understand how this is possible." I turned to face Matthew.

Matthew shrugged slightly. "Their best guess is that even though **he's** an incorporeal being and not visible to the naked eye, light interacts with **him** in the same way that it does us. It bounces off **him** just like it bounces off you and me. There's no way to test the theory of course, but it does make a certain amount of sense."

"Does it?" I pulled a face; physics had not been my best subject in school.

"It does. Of course, if **he'd** only—"

"Why don't you ever call him Blake?"

Despite the fact that I'd interrupted, Matthew seemed quite willing to answer my question. "**He** doesn't have a name. Or a title for that matter. I assumed you'd decided to call him Blake."

"No, that's his name. And what do you mean, he doesn't have a title? Of course he does. You do know who he is, don't you?" I was puzzled by what Matthew was saying.

Matthew stilled beside me. "All I know is that he can open a portal to both Heaven and Hell."

"That's all you know?" I frowned at Matthew.

"Well… I'm sure you know the rest."

"Not really. I've not had anyone to talk to about any of this," I lied. "Apart from him, that is." I purposely avoided using Blake's name in a bid to win Matthew over.

Matthew studied me for a moment, scepticism written all over his face. Eventually he seemed to believe me. "Why not? Maybe it will make the ritual easier for you to bear." He paused, glancing upwards, perhaps gathering his thoughts, debating exactly what it was that he was allowed to tell me. "Aeons ago, one of your ancestors stole a piece of **his** soul. She was the first Key, and in doing what she did, she forced **him** to remain in spirit form, unable to open the portal. The demons were divided, locked in their own dimensions. Ever since then, my family has been keeping an eye on each Key in turn, waiting for the day that she started to control **him**. It was always going to happen, you see. The lure of all that power was irresistible." Matthew paused, but then added, "I *am* sorry that you're the one who's fallen victim to its charms. I was actually getting quite fond of you." He shrugged again. "Anyway, only when the Key started to control **him** could the ritual be performed."

"Matthew, that's… utter bollocks." How had Matthew been duped into believing such nonsense? He sounded almost sympathetic to the plight of the demons.

"You would say that. It was your ancestor that stole a piece of **his** soul."

"No, they didn't."

Matthew only stared at me.

"Honestly, Matthew, they didn't. The original Keeper of Souls—"

"Keeper of Souls?"

"That's his title, Matthew. That's his purpose. He reaps the souls of the dying, preserving the energy of creation."

Matthew pulled a face, but I soldiered on with my explanation.

"His father fell in love with a human, but he couldn't conceive a child with her. Instead, he gave her his soul. The soul split in two, one part forming a child in her womb, the other part forming Blake. I have the soul now because it's been passed down through the generations until I was born. My ancestors didn't steal it."

"You expect me to believe that? A being second only to God fell in love with a nobody? Come on, Emma," Matthew scoffed.

"It's true, I had a vision. I saw it with my own eyes."

"The soul is clearly making you delusional. No wonder you've started to want more. Perhaps it's for the best that they'll be doing the ritual soon."

"Matthew! You have to believe me." I reached out to take hold of his arm, but Matthew only brushed me away and pulled me down the rest of the stairs.

Chapter 14 – Emma
Sunday 2nd June 2019

The gardens that Matthew and I wandered around were beautiful, and it was nice to be outside, but my mind was elsewhere. Matthew had clearly been duped, but by who? His father? Did he know the truth about Blake? Or had the whole family been deceived by demons? While I pondered these questions and more, a truly disturbing thought occurred. Had Matthew's family willingly formed an alliance with the demons? Had they been spying on my ancestors for centuries because they wanted to? Or because they had to?

I knew that there was no point asking Matthew my questions, but I couldn't seem to help myself. "Matthew," I started, realising that I couldn't exactly ask what I wanted to. I didn't think he'd respond all that well to me asking why he was being such a prat. "Why do you think the demons want the portal opening?"

"Excuse me?" Matthew replied, somewhat distracted. Evidently he'd been lost in thought too. I couldn't help but wonder what he'd been thinking about. I knew that he didn't believe my version of events, but maybe I'd at least got him to question some of what he'd been told.

"The portal," I prompted. "Why do you think they want it opened?"

"They want to be reunited with their brethren."

"Do you really believe that's all they want?"

"Don't you?"

"No, Matthew. No, I don't. I think that they want their freedom, all right. But when they have it, they'll want control of Earth. They'll start a war with the angels, and we'll suffer the consequences."

"I don't think so, Emma."

"So... they've... erm, they've never killed anyone?"

"Of course they've killed people. Sacrifice is necessary. There's power in taking a life."

"Matthew..." I gasped before my voice trailed off. Matthew was happily condoning murder as if it were nothing. I just couldn't wrap my head around it; I couldn't reconcile the Matthew that I'd worked alongside, the one that everybody had loved, with the Matthew who stood before me now. He'd been so nice, but then he'd kidnapped me. He'd seemed to care about me, bringing me food, drink, and toiletries, arranging for me to have some time outside, but then he'd just dismissed the ultimate crime.

I clamped my mouth shut and fell in step alongside him while my brain worked on overtime. While I'd been asking questions, it had decided—all by itself, I might add—that this might be my one and only chance to escape. I was outside after all; half the job had been done for me. Consciously I'd given up on being able to free myself. I mean, let's be honest, I wasn't exactly the best placed to fight my way out of any given situation, and while I hadn't seen anyone other than Matthew, I assumed there were guards. I didn't think I'd come out on top against someone who carried a gun, or even a knife, not when the only thing I'd found to arm myself with was the remote control for a television. Obviously my unconscious self had simply disagreed with my conclusions and carried on plotting.

Trying to be discreet about it, I glanced around at my surroundings. I still had no idea where I was, although I was relieved to find that I was in a house at least, a very big house but still just a house. The gardens were enormous; we'd been walking for a while and still hadn't reached a boundary marker of any kind.

"How big is this place?" The words popped out before I could stop them.

"Big enough. Why do you ask?" Drat! Matthew was on to me. My heart skipped a beat and then started to race.

"No real reason," I replied as nonchalantly as I could. "I was just making conversation, as you do." I kept my face turned away from Matthew because I could feel my cheeks reddening. "I mean, *my* house is only a little two-up, two-down so this is… well, quite unexpected," I finished. *Unexpected?* I berated myself.

"It's been in the family for generations," Matthew supplied without any further comment.

"Lovely," I remarked, trying to sound innocent despite accepting that my brain might be onto something. Not that I was getting very far with my scheming. It was all well and good for my brain to decide that this was my chance to leg it, but it hadn't really worked out the practicalities of doing so. I was handcuffed to Matthew after all, and while I could think of several ways to escape from that predicament, none of them were all that appealing. Gnawing through my own wrist didn't sound like so much fun. Then again, neither did being used in some kind of ritual that I assumed would result in my death. I really was in a pickle.

A wave of panic engulfed me whole. What the hell was I going to do? Other than die of course. My emotions spiked again, although this time despair was intermingled with terror, and love had threaded its way through the despair. Wait a second… love? I wasn't starting to have romantic feelings towards Matthew, was I? I knew all about Stockholm Syndrome of course but… surely not? I mean, I knew Matthew was handsome. In fact, he was gorgeous, but he was one of the bad guys, and personally I didn't think the sharp suit worked for him. Matthew, with his unruly mop of sandy blonde hair and piercing blue eyes, was meant for the casual look. He looked good in chinos, with a shirt hanging loosely over his shoulders, the sleeves rolled up to his elbows. He suited the woven bracelets that usually adorned his wrist and the wooden beads that normally hung around his neck. The tailored look didn't really work for him. Some men could pull it off, some men couldn't. Matthew was one of those who couldn't. Now Blake, on the other hand, he could pull it off. In fact, he looked delicious in a tux.

I'd only seen Blake dressed up once, and only briefly, but the memory was enough to make me smile despite my circumstances. He'd shown up ready for our first date dressed as though I was taking him to an extravagant ball and not just the local pub. Of course, he'd quickly changed, but that brief glimpse of him in his finery had triggered a bow wave of lust in me that had my cheeks reddening even now. And he'd looked even better in jeans and a white shirt. I had a thing for a man in jeans and a white shirt, especially if the shirt was a nice thick cotton one.

No, I definitely wasn't falling for Matthew because I was in love with Blake… whose emotions I could feel if he was close enough to me. Why hadn't that thought occurred until now?

Blake, I screamed in my head. *Blake!*

Why wasn't he answering me? If I could feel his emotions, and I was sure they were his now that the thought had occurred, I should be able to talk to him. I should have been able to pull him to me all along. What was wrong with me? Had I been drugged with something that blocked our connection? Was that even possible?

Blake, I sobbed, concentrating on my own emotions, hoping that he could feel me at least, even if he couldn't hear me. I was desperate for him to know how much I loved him. He was my everything. I'd heard others say that their partners completed them, but in mine and Blake's case, it really was true. We shared a soul, we were half of a whole, nothing without the other. He was mine, and I was his.

A sharp pain shot through my right eye, forcing me to cry out. Without thinking, I lifted both of my hands to my head, forcing Matthew's hand to follow along with my own.

"Emma—" he started to say. I could hear the irritation in his voice, but I was already falling to the ground. My knees simply gave way and crumpled beneath me.

"Blake," I mumbled, not thinking or caring about Matthew. I pushed the heel of my palm into the corner of my eye, hoping that pressure would even out the pain and reduce the intensity. A sharp spike had been driven into my skull; fire was dancing across my nerve endings.

"Emma!" Matthew gasped. "You're bleeding."

I didn't need Matthew to be more specific; it was another nosebleed, what else would it be? Despite the pain, I brushed my free hand across my face. Yep, it was another nosebleed, a big one judging by the amount of blood smeared across the back of my hand.

"Help!" I heard Matthew calling out to whoever else was on the estate, but I was closing down, my eyes were failing, and I was happy to let darkness overtake me. Wouldn't it be ironic if I died now, just before the new moon, before they could do whatever it was that they'd nabbed me for? "Emma, stay with me," Matthew said, sounding genuinely concerned.

But I could save the world by dying, I thought, laughing softly to myself. At least I think I laughed to myself. I wanted to tell Matthew to 'do one,' but I couldn't force the words out. Instead, I concentrated on Blake. If I really was dying, I wanted my last thoughts to be of him.

"What the fuck happened here?" A new voice sounded above me, a harsh voice. Nasty.

"I don't know. She just collapsed," Matthew answered. All traces of concern had left his voice. Instead, he sounded deferential. Clearly the newcomer was higher up the food chain than he was.

I know what happened. It's the power of the soul—it's killing me. I couldn't help myself from answering them in the silence of my mind. Even if I'd wanted to join in their conversation, I didn't have the energy to do anything other than listen. The pain was all-consuming.

"Get the cuffs off her. Quickly, boy. Do it!"

Matthew didn't answer, but I felt the weight of the handcuffs being removed from my wrist. *I'm free,* I thought. Now if only I could force my body to roll over so that I could pull myself upright and run. I struggled to move, and I must have managed to do something because a weight was placed on my shoulders, pushing me back to the ground.

"No, don't, Emma. You'll only make it worse," Matthew said. It almost sounded like he cared.

Worse! How could it possibly be any worse? I've been kidnapped, and I'm being held hostage. I'm going to be used in a ritual that will bring about the end of the world. Or else, I'm going to die here and now.

Oh pfft, stop feeling so sorry for yourself, Johnna interrupted my moaning.

Johnna! I gasped. *I'm not dead.*

Not yet. And I suspect these goons will save you. They need you alive, don't they?

Sure enough, I felt my body being lifted into the air. I hoped it was Matthew who held me close because while he obviously had a suspect moral code, at least I'd liked him once upon a time. Whoever owned the new voice was not a good person. I could tell that from the way that he'd spoken to Matthew, from the venom that I'd heard in his voice. I didn't want him cradling my body into his. Matthew was a poor substitute for Blake, but if I couldn't have Blake, Matthew was better than Mr. Nasty.

Blake is out there, Johnna remarked.

It was him that I felt then. I breathed a sigh of relief, grateful to have what I'd known to be true confirmed by someone else.

Of course it was him. Who else could it be?

Johnna, I asked, changing the subject, *what's going to happen now?*

I imagine they'll hook you up to a drip. I'm hoping they won't pump you full of drugs. They shouldn't; they don't know what they're dealing with. And then we wait for Ellie.

And Blake?

Come on, Emma, wake up! Blake can't enter this place. That's why he hasn't answered any of your calls.

But... Blake can go anywhere.
Anywhere that hasn't been warded.
Warded?
Yes, the runes.
The runes?
Emma, I know you're mostly unconscious at the minute, but you really need to start thinking for yourself, Johnna chided. *The runes that are painted around the top of your room and along the hallway. Most of them are designed to keep spirits away. They're probably all over the building.*

I decided to ignore Johnna's rebuke. I figured I had every right to be slow at the minute. Instead, I asked a question. *But how do you know what they say?*

John knew the languages of both the angels and the demons. That means I know them too.

But... John's dead.
So am I, but here we are.
I don't understand.
Emma, you really do need to start paying attention to the things I tell you. The golden soul is unchanging, remember?
And?
And in the same way that my spirit became fused with the soul, John's did too.

John's in there? No wonder my own head felt so crowded sometimes.

He's here, Johnna confirmed.

That's how you were able to read the prophecy then. I smiled. Johnna's cryptic half hints were starting to make sense at long last. Before I could ask anything else, a stinging sensation roused me.

"Hey!" Mr. Nasty slapped me across the face. "Wake up."

"Ngargh," I muttered, trying to force my eyelids apart. They seemed to be glued shut, so instead I opted for swatting Mr. Nasty away, but I found that I didn't have full control of my limbs yet. In my head, I was beautifully coordinated, but to be honest, I barely managed to raise my hand up.

"Stop that! You'll hurt her." It was nice to know that Matthew was still willing to defend me, even if he was also willing to sacrifice me.

"How dare you?" Mr. Nasty spat. Poor Matthew. While I didn't condone his behaviour, and it was entirely possible that he deserved everything he got and more, I felt a wave of sympathy for him.

"I'm sorry, Father," Matthew muttered so quietly that I almost didn't catch it.

Father?! I exclaimed silently.

"Remember your place, boy," Mr. Nasty—Matthew had told her his name was Terrance—continued.

"Yes, Father."

"Ngargh," I said again, wanting to intervene on Matthew's behalf.

"It's okay, Emma." Matthew took hold of my hand, stroking it gently with his thumb. "You're going to be okay."

"She'd better be, boy. We've not waited this long for you to bugger it up by killing her now."

"But Father…" Matthew started to say, but he was cut off by the slamming of a door.

Chapter 15 – Ellie
Monday 3rd June 2019

Ellie wandered aimlessly around Scott's workshop, randomly picking things up before absently putting them back down somewhere else.

"Do you want to talk about it?" Scott asked. He was standing at the forge, working on a piece of iron, his face ruddy from the heat of the fire.

"What's there to talk about?" Ellie sounded morose.

"Oh, I don't know…" Scott glanced up from what he was doing. "The fact that my sister's been kidnapped. The fact that if we don't do something about it, she's going to die. The fact that Abaddon's plan sucks."

"I still can't believe it." Tears welled up in Ellie's eyes.

Scott laid aside the piece that he was working on and crossed the room to where Ellie was standing.

"I thought it was bad for the metal if you put it down," Ellie mumbled.

"I can always start again if I need to," Scott replied, wrapping his arms around Ellie. Ellie couldn't be certain because she couldn't see Scott's face, but from how his body started to quake, she guessed that he'd started to cry too.

"How are your mum and dad doing?" Ellie asked after some time had passed.

Scott huffed and gently shook his head from side to side, but he didn't release his hold on Ellie. "How do you think?" His voice was thick with emotion.

"If I had to guess," Ellie pulled away from Scott so that she could look him in the eye, "your mum's busy making posters…" she paused briefly before continuing, "…and your dad's barely functioning. He's probably at Emma's more than he is at home, notionally feeding Cooper and Watson."

"That's about right, but Mum's with Dad at Emma's. I think

they only go home to sleep."

"We should have gone to stay with them really."

"Maybe, but then we wouldn't have been able to work with Blake or Abaddon. Besides, I've rung them every couple of hours, and your mum and dad are there quite a lot."

"At Emma's?" Ellie couldn't keep the surprise from her voice. Scott nodded.

"Cooper and Watson won't be happy then," Ellie remarked. "They don't like strangers."

"Your mum and dad aren't strangers."

"They are to Cooper and Watson."

"Have you spoken to them at all? Your mum and dad, that is?"

"A few times, but they didn't say anything about being at Emma's."

"What did they say?"

"Dad said I could move back home until Emma was found if I wanted to, but Mum knows this is it and that I need to…" Ellie paused, searching for the right words, "…do something. She's terrified because her worst fears are coming true."

"Hey, it's okay." Scott bent forwards and kissed Ellie's forehead. "Abaddon's plan will work."

"You just said it sucked."

"Well… yeah okay, it does suck, but it's the only plan we've got. Look," Scott changed the subject, "I really do need to make the knives that Abaddon said we'd need."

"Okay." Ellie rubbed her face, wiping away the last of her tears. "Can I help?"

"It's dangerous."

"So is what we're planning to do next," Ellie remarked.

Scott frowned. "Yeah, I guess it is," he replied. "You'll need to put one of those on then." He pointed towards the door, on the back of which was a row of hooks. Hanging from each one was a leather apron.

"What do we do first?" Ellie asked while doing as Scott had instructed.

"Well, Abaddon was quite specific about the fact that the knives needed to be made of iron. So, first of all, we melt some iron."

Ellie nodded, remembering that Abaddon had indeed said something about iron being able to disrupt the flow of magic.

"Here," Scott handed Ellie a pair of what looked like barbecue tongs. "Use these to pick that up." He pointed at a clay bowl filled with lumps of iron. "And then put it in here." He pulled down a hatch on the side of the forge.

A blast of heat warmed Ellie's face. "How hot is it in there?" she asked.

"Hot enough to melt iron," Scott answered.

"Okay, now what?" Ellie pulled the barbecue tongs out from the forge so that Scott could close the hatch again.

"There isn't a great deal more to do really. I've got some moulds already that will suffice."

Ellie turned and looked up at Scott. "Why've you got knife moulds?"

"Because I'm a blacksmith."

"But I thought you made gates and railings... that sort of thing."

"Mostly, but I make knives too." Scott turned away from Ellie so that he could find the moulds he'd mentioned. "And the occasional sword," he said over his shoulder.

"Swords!" Ellie exclaimed, her eyes turning into mini saucers.

"If it can be made with metal, I've made it," Scott replied, still grubbing about for the moulds. When he eventually found them, he set them down on a concrete slab at the end of his workbench.

"What's the concrete for?" Ellie asked, although she was still thinking about the fact that Scott had made any number of swords.

"It absorbs the heat from the iron so that the workbench doesn't catch fire."

"Oh." There wasn't much more that Ellie could say to that.

"You okay?" Scott asked, glancing over his shoulder at Ellie.

"Yes, I'm fine."

Scott smiled, not that it reached his eyes. "You're not really, are you?"

"No," Ellie shook her head, "but then again, neither are you."

"No, I'm not. I still can't believe this is happening either."

Both Ellie and Scott fell silent while Scott lined up the moulds. When he'd finished and they were neatly in a row, he opened up the forge and carefully lifted out the clay pot.

"I thought making a knife would be harder than this," Ellie

commented.

"It depends on the knife. And we're not finished yet. We need to let them cool, and then we need to sharpen and polish them."

"Didn't Abaddon say we had to carve a symbol on each one too?"

"She did, yes." Scott was concentrating on pouring the molten iron into the moulds.

"How long will they take to go hard?" Ellie asked.

"If we left them to cool down on their own, all day."

"But we don't have all day," Ellie argued.

"No, we don't." Scott lifted the first mould up with a funny-shaped tool that allowed him to grip it from the top. Once he had it securely in his grasp, he carefully lowered it into a bucket of water. It hissed and sizzled with the venom of a cobra.

When the knives were cool enough to handle, Scott smashed each of the moulds and then reached for another tool. "You can help with this bit if you want," he said to Ellie. "We need to sharpen the blades and then polish them up."

"Why not?" Ellie agreed.

It took a few hours, but eventually they had four identical knives. Each one was made from a single piece of metal and had a smooth rounded handle and a sharp pointed blade. Scott then did the work to carve Abaddon's symbol into each one.

When the first knife was finished, Ellie took it from Scott and lifted it up to the light. "It looks like a capital A," she remarked.

"Not quite." Scott was concentrating on the second blade. He'd already etched the sloping sides of the 'A' into the iron and had started work on the bar that went across the middle of the 'A'. It looked like an unfinished infinity sign.

"Do you think this is Abaddon's personal brand?"

"I don't know. She said it was a protection symbol."

"Abaddon says a lot of things."

Scott glanced at Ellie before turning back to the knife he was working on. "Don't you trust her?"

"I do, of course I do. Emma doesn't though."

"Emma doesn't trust anyone until they've proven themselves. Besides, Abaddon was in favour of killing Emma."

"I know." Ellie sighed, placing the knife that she was holding back onto the workbench. "I wish she was here."

"Emma or Abaddon?"

"Emma."

"That makes two of us. Then we wouldn't have to break into a demon house to save her."

"I hope she's okay."

"We have to trust that she is. Blake would've let us know if anything had happened to her."

"But he'd only know if she'd died."

"Don't do that to yourself, Ellie. Don't go borrowing trouble."

"It's hard not to at the minute."

"I know."

"Are you scared?" Ellie asked, abruptly changing the subject.

Scott placed the last of the knives on the workbench and turned to face Ellie. "I'm bloody terrified. I barely had time to get used to the idea of the supernatural and now…" His voice trailed off into nothing.

"You don't have to come with me if you don't want," Ellie said, but she couldn't quite keep the wobble out of her voice.

"Ellie." Scott's voice was firm. "I'm coming with you, and that's the end of it."

"There will be demons."

"I know."

"And we might die."

"I know that, too."

"But—"

"No buts, Ellie. Abaddon's plan is the only one we've got. We're going to see it through, and we're going to get my sister back before anything can happen to her."

"Okay." Ellie heaved a sigh of relief and straightened her spine. "We're really doing this then… together."

"We are. If you think I'm letting you out of my sight, you've got another thing coming. I'm scared for Emma. I'd be inconsolable if it were you."

A brief smile lifted the corner of Ellie's lips. "Well, then," she said, "if we're really doing it, we should probably go."

Chapter 16 – Ellie
Monday 3rd June 2019

"Are you sure about this?" Ellie asked Scott despite their earlier conversation, her eyes boring into the red brick wall in front of her.

"I've already told you that I am," Scott replied. He was standing next to Ellie, but instead of staring directly ahead, he was watching the sun sink behind the horizon.

Ellie bit her lip before speaking again. "I should go in on my own. Because of Abaddon's gifts, I'm faster than you are, I'm stronger than you are. I—"

"Ellie." Scott turned and placed his hands on her shoulders, gently manoeuvring her around until they were facing each other. "You're the love of my life; I'm not letting you face a horde of demons without me."

"But—"

"No buts, Ellie." Scott's hands slid down Ellie's shoulders. He pulled her close and then gently kissed her on the lips. "Now then! That's all the incentive I need to make it out of there alive," he declared when they broke apart.

"Me too," Ellie agreed, a slight smile lifting the corners of her mouth.

"So," Scott drew in a deep breath, exhaled loudly, and then continued, "it's as easy as scale the wall, cross the grounds, break into the house, and destroy the ruby."

"And don't get caught," Ellie added wryly.

"And don't get caught," Scott agreed, nodding his head.

Abaddon's plan had been surprisingly simple, but it relied on Ellie and Scott more than anyone else. They had to be the ones to break into the demon house because neither angels nor spectral beings could enter. According to Abaddon, demons used runes to keep out unwanted guests, so until Ellie and Scott had disrupted the magic of the runes they were on their own. To do that, they had to find and destroy the power source using an iron blade. Abaddon believed that it would be a ruby because demons had been using rubies for centuries to power their magic. The problem was that Abaddon was only guessing, and even if she was right, she couldn't tell Ellie or Scott where the ruby would be. Her only advice was that it was probably somewhere central.

Ellie took a deep breath and straightened her spine. "Let's do this then," she said, putting one foot on the bottom of the ladder that was leaning against the wall. Abaddon hadn't been able to do much for them—she hadn't even been able to ascertain if the demons employed any security measures other than the runes—but she had been able to conjure up a ladder to help Ellie and Scott get over the first obstacle.

It didn't take long for Ellie to hop over the wall, and Scott was quick to follow, but whereas Ellie landed with the grace of a cat, Scott fell to the ground with a thump.

"Scott!" Ellie hissed, instinctively dropping into a slight crouch. "Are you okay?"

"Just peachy," Scott muttered, a slight flush warming his face.

Ellie let the matter drop, not wanting to hurt Scott's pride. She glanced around, trying to get her bearings while Scott clambered to his feet, brushing the dirt from his trousers. "The house should be straight ahead," Ellie whispered, in part to herself. A quick internet search earlier on in the day had brought up aerial shots of the estate.

Scott didn't answer. Instead, he took hold of Ellie's hand, and together they started weaving their way through the dense woodland that they'd found themselves in, pushing past overgrown ferns and climbing over rotting logs that lay where they'd fallen. By the time the trees had started to thin out, both of them were hot and sweaty.

"They don't seem to care much about the landscaping, do they?" Scott remarked, coming to a halt.

Ellie shrugged her shoulders. "Maybe it's a security measure?"

Scott shook his head. "Woodland isn't all that defensible because you rarely get a clear line of sight. That's the security measure." Scott pointed up ahead.

"Dammit!" Ellie cursed. In front of them was a second stone wall. This one was curved and appeared to serve only as a barrier between the mass of foliage that was now behind them and the rest of the estate. It wasn't the wall that was the problem though. "We can't cross that," Ellie continued, stabbing a finger at what lay beyond, a vast expanse of manicured lawn. "We'll be seen."

Scott chewed on a fingernail before answering. "This way," he replied, turning to the right, making the decision based on nothing but gut instinct.

Ellie nodded and followed along behind him, but the anxiety that she'd been holding onto all day swelled in her gut.

After only a short walk, Scott spoke up again. "We can use that for cover." He pointed at a line of perfectly trimmed box hedges that ran from the wall over towards the house. "It's a privet, I think."

Ellie only nodded before starting to climb the wall. It had been made by nestling uneven chunks of grey slate together, secured in place with nothing more than moss. She found it an easy climb, as did Scott, and together they ran the length of the hedge. It towered above them, easily standing at over eight feet tall. When it came to an end, Ellie, who was in the lead, peeked around the corner, obviously triggering a sensor somewhere because flood lights lit up the garden, chasing away the shadows that dusk had started to usher in. All of Ellie's doubt and fear exploded outwards. Her heart rate spiked as she ducked back behind the hedge, pushing herself into the privet. "We need to hide," she hissed at Scott.

"This way." Scott grabbed Ellie's hand and pulled her back the way they'd come. "I think I saw something."

"Hush, wait a second." Ellie stopped, pulling her hand free from Scott's.

"What is it?"

"Somebody's arguing."

Scott strained but heard nothing.

"Oh! That's not good for us." The blood drained from Ellie's face. "What are we going to do?"

"What did you hear?"

"They're sending someone out to search the grounds."

"Come on, this way." Scott took off again. About halfway along the hedge, he'd spotted a neatly shaped archway. "It must be a maze," he said. "Perhaps it will take us straight to the house?"

"Well, we can't go that way." Ellie glanced over her shoulder. "From what I saw, there's nothing to hide behind. It's just a big patio."

"The maze it is then."

"But what if we get lost in there?"

"I don't think it's all that big. I'm sure we can manage."

"I suppose," Ellie conceded, her brow furrowed.

Scott pressed a kiss to Ellie's forehead. "Look, why don't we get at least some of the way in there," he pointed forwards, "so that whoever's out there," he indicated behind him, "doesn't find us, and then we'll regroup."

Ellie bit her lip before nodding, finally accepting that there wasn't an alternative. "Okay," she said, plunging into the shadows, turning left and right at random, trusting that Scott was keeping up. She was about to comment that they were lost when she glimpsed an opening ahead; they'd found the centre of the maze. "It's actually quite nice, isn't it?" she remarked, glancing over her shoulder at Scott, who only shrugged.

The hedges had been trimmed so as to leave an open space, in the centre of which was a raised circular pond with a stone ledge running around its perimeter. It was filled with koi carp and had an elevated dais in the middle that served as both a bird bath and a fountain. It was the perfect resting place.

Scott ignored the scenery in favour of his phone. "Let's see if we can find a way out of here." He called up the aerial shots that they'd looked at earlier on. "It's difficult to see, but I think I've got it. What do you think?" He offered his phone to Ellie, who was staring at the fish, watching them swim lazily around in circles, disappearing underneath a set of lily pads on one side of the pond only to re-emerge moments later on the other side of the pond. There was at least a dozen of them, ranging in size and colour. Most of them had white bodies that were covered in orange splotches, but there was a particularly attractive one that was a patchwork of black and orange.

"They're pretty, aren't they?" Ellie nodded towards the fish. "You wouldn't think that demons would bother with all of this, would you?"

"Maybe this is for the people who live here." Scott shrugged, looking again at his phone.

"You think people live here too?"

"I guess. I don't know." Scott let his phone drop and looked over at Ellie. "What's wrong? Other than the obvious, that is?"

Ellie refused to meet his eye. "I don't know… I mean, I guess I just didn't think about running into anyone. I only thought about the demons, but back there…" Ellie glanced over her shoulder. "…and now this. What if we have to kill someone?"

"We won't."

"You don't know that."

"You're right, I don't. But I do know you. You won't hurt anyone just for the sake of it."

"But what if—"

"Ellie, you won't. But if you're worried about it, you stay here. I'll go in on my own."

"No, I can't let you do that. I just… I didn't think, that's all, and I don't like the idea of killing someone."

"Well, let's make sure it doesn't come to that."

Ellie's mouth curved upwards into a smile, but it didn't reach her eyes. "We might not have a choice."

"We might not," Scott agreed, before adding, "but we can do our utmost to avoid getting into a fight. With people anyway. I don't know about you, but I'm good with the idea of killing demons."

Ellie breathed deeply before nodding. "Okay, you're right. I'm being silly, aren't I? We've come this far, we can't exactly chicken out now."

"You're not being silly." Scott wrapped his arms around her, his phone still held tightly in his hand. "You're being you, and that's just one of the reasons why I love you so damn much."

Ellie huffed but didn't make any effort to leave the safety of Scott's arms. "I suppose we'd best get moving then. What time is it anyway?"

"It's almost eleven. We've only got an hour or so to spare, if the ritual is performed at midnight, that is."

"Urgh, come on then." Ellie finally broke free. "Did you find a route through the maze?"

"I think so. I think it's this way." Scott pointed towards one of the archways that had been cut into the hedge. They'd come through one on their way into the centre of the maze, but Scott pointed at one on their left. "It's logical at least because that one looks like it leads towards the house."

"Then lead on, kind sir." Ellie gestured for Scott to go in front of her.

The walk through the remainder of the maze was uneventful. Scott paused frequently to check his 'map,' weaving his way ever closer to the monster of a house that loomed overhead, and eventually arriving at a plain wooden door. "This is it," he whispered, grasping hold of the handle.

"It will be locked, won't it?"

Scott pushed downwards. "It's not." He inched the door open, waiting for someone to say something. When no one did, he glanced back at Ellie before taking a step over the threshold.

Chapter 17 – Emma
Monday 3rd June 2019

"Emma." A voice sounded in the distance. I was either drugged or dying. Either way, I couldn't summon up the energy to give a crap. All I felt was tired. Stray thoughts wandered in and out of my mind at will, offering me tantalising glimpses of things that I should probably care about, but when I tried to pin them down, they dissipated into the ether.

"Emma!" The voice sounded again. "Come on, Emma. I need you to wake up." I tried, I really did, but my body and I were disconnected, two separate entities occupying the same space. And then something icy cold and wet was laid on my forehead.

The cool material was reviving; it reminded me that I'd been kidnapped, that I'd collapsed, that I was most likely about to die, but that before I would be left alone to die in peace, I was going to be used in a ritual that would bring about the end of the earth. Well, maybe it wasn't quite that dramatic, Earth would probably survive. It would probably continue along its merry little way for billions of millennia yet, orbiting the sun as it always had. But mankind would certainly suffer. Mankind would be forced to share the earth with demons. And with angels but, let's be honest about this, it was the demons that bothered me the most. Who knew that demons really existed? That God was real, and that long before he'd thought about creating us, he'd created two entirely different races—the angels and the demons.

"I know you're awake," Matthew said. Even though I hadn't opened my eyes, I knew it was him who'd been trying to rouse me. My senses were slowly returning; I was no longer swimming in darkness, and sounds were becoming more distinct. Still, I kept my eyes closed, hoping that eventually he'd just leave. "You need to get changed."

Why would I need to get changed? I wondered, pulling a face.

"I saw that," Matthew remarked.

Drat! I thought before peeking at Matthew from underneath my eyelashes. "Why do I need to get changed?" I croaked.

"Here, let me get you a drink." Matthew turned away for a brief moment before setting a glass of water on the bedside cabinet. "Do you need help sitting up?"

I wanted to say no, to tell him to shove it so far up his backside that only surgery would get it out. But I couldn't, because while my mind was definitely clearing, my body still felt too heavy. It felt like I'd overdone it in the garden, every single muscle ached, even the non-skeletal ones, and so I nodded.

"Is it drugged?" I asked while Matthew helped me up.

"No."

"But you have been drugging me, haven't you?" My voice sounded hoarse, damaged even.

"I have. You needed medication."

A bark-like sound escaped from my mouth, and I shook my head gently. "Medication? Is that what we're calling it now?"

"That's what it was. You were dying. For all I know, you're still dying. But you have to get up and get changed." Matthew offered me the glass.

"So you've said." I took a drink. "How long have I been out?"

"Just over twenty-four hours."

Twenty-four hours! How could I have let twenty-four hours slide by? I should have been trying to escape. Not that my first attempt had been even a little bit successful. But I should have tried again.

I took another sip of water, holding it in my mouth before swallowing, enjoying the cooling sensation as it washed down my throat.

"Do you want me to put the shower on for you?" Matthew interrupted my musing.

"I'm not having a shower. And I'm not getting changed. I'm staying right here," I declared, my voice stronger than it had been only moments before.

"If you don't get up voluntarily, you know that I'll be forced to take action."

Hmmm… I did indeed know that Matthew could—and would—use whatever force was necessary to make me comply, but was he being forced himself? After our excursion, after seeing the way that his father treated him, I couldn't help but wonder. "Matthew…?" The question was implied. "Why are you doing all of this?"

"You know why." Matthew turned away and strode off into the

bathroom. Much as I didn't want to get into the habit of following his orders, I found myself pushing the bedcovers to one side and following him. Every single joint in my body protested at the movement, and when I glanced down, I wasn't at all surprised to see a bruise on the back of my hand, another in the crook of my elbow, and finger marks snaking their way around my upper arm. Whoever had administered the 'medication' had certainly not been gentle.

"You don't still believe what you've been told, do you?" I asked. I knew Matthew had been lied to, but surely he'd started to question his beliefs? He'd treated me so tenderly and with such kindness that I was starting to think Matthew the Vet wasn't entirely a fictional creation.

Matthew stilled. He was facing away from me, so I couldn't see his face, but he straightened his spine and his body tensed. "Honestly, Emma, I don't know what to think, but I do know that my father will kill me if you're not downstairs in the next hour looking reasonably presentable. I'm the heir; I do as I'm told." He stopped speaking for a moment before adding, "Besides which, if I don't make you presentable, my father will only send one of the others. And the others don't care about you, not at all. You'll be beaten, stripped, hosed down, and then forced to the ritual site."

There was no way to answer that, so I didn't. "Get out then," I said, accepting that I might as well shower. The idea of being 'hosed down' wasn't all that appealing, and if my options were limited to having a wash by myself or being washed by someone else, then I was going to choose option A.

When I came out of the bathroom, wrapped in only a towel, Matthew had made the bed and laid out a fresh set of clothes. He was standing by the window.

"No way, Matthew," I said, after only a quick glance at what I was supposed to wear.

"My father says you either wear that or you go to the ritual naked. His preference is that you go naked."

"Matthew…" I couldn't help myself from whining. The clothes that had been laid out for me would have made a hooker look decent. Without knowing where it came from, I flashed back to the dream that Ellie had had a few days ago. The clothes that she'd described weren't exactly the same as the ones that Matthew expected me to wear, but they were of the same ilk. The top was dark red and while spaghetti straps would hold it in place, the material was so sheer that it would leave nothing to the imagination. And the skirt… well, it was long, but the twin splits up either side would undoubtedly expose my knicker line. I felt sick to my stomach wondering what else from Ellie's dream was going to come true, or true enough.

"I don't know what to tell you, Emma. It's either that or nothing."

"I could keep my old clothes on."

Matthew shook his head. "No, Emma, you can't. I took them away while you were getting cleaned up."

"You came into the bathroom while I was in the shower?" I asked. And only a moment ago I'd been thinking that Matthew might actually be one of the good guys.

"I did. I had to." Matthew held my gaze despite the fact that if looks could kill, he'd be six feet under. Not once did his eyeline drop to my chest or lower.

"Fine." Anger burned in my veins. "I'll keep the towel on then." At least the towel wasn't see-through, even if it was a little shorter than I would have liked.

"I can't let you do that." Matthew pulled his shirt cuffs straight before clasping his hands loosely in front of his body. He looked particularly smart in an all-black suit that brought to mind Blake's preferred attire, but whereas Blake's dress was reminiscent of bygone times, Matthew looked sharp, ultra modern. "I'll turn my back if you want."

"I think that's the least you can do," I spat, opting to get dressed as opposed to wearing nothing, not that either choice was particularly palatable. How on God's green earth had I ended up here? Willingly getting ready to be sacrificed? But if I didn't go willingly, I would only be forced, and I suspected that that would hurt a whole lot more. I wasn't all that enamoured with the idea of experiencing any more pain, not that I wanted the end of the world either, but I was quickly running out of options.

Johnna, I called out silently.
I'm here, child. I'll always be here.
What do I do?
Trust in Ellie.
Ellie isn't here. She can't save me; no one can. No one knows where I am.

Is that right?

You know it is.

Well then, trust in yourself. You'll know what to do when the time is right.

That isn't very helpful.

Do you remember what Jennifer told you?

Of course I do. She told me that I was the Key and that I could control Blake.

Well, there you go then.

"Cryptic as always," I muttered out loud.

"What was that?" Matthew asked, turning around.

"Nothing."

"I see you're ready."

"I didn't really have a choice, did I?" I remarked. And sadly it hadn't taken me much time to get ready. Both the top and the skirt had been easy enough to pull on. My only opportunity for stalling had been when I'd done my hair, not that my hair mattered, but I hadn't wanted it in my eyes. Although perhaps I should have left it down, it might have been useful to hide behind. Yes, I know, I was grasping at straws, but did I really want to see what was coming?

"Let's go then. You'll need to be handcuffed to me again."

I glared at Matthew before offering him my arm. And before I knew it, we were descending a set of stone steps down into what I assumed was the basement of the house. It seemed Ellie had got the location right when she'd dreamt about my future. Fear and anger fought for supremacy. There was no escaping the fact that I was terrified. My heart would have won top spot in the grand prix if it had been a part of the race, my mouth tasted like the Sahara, and my body was trembling so hard that my knees were literally knocking together. But I was also furious, and I was holding tightly onto the fury in the hope that it would see me through whatever was about to happen. It had served me well in the past after all.

Matthew led me into what appeared to be an underground chamber, based on the fact that there were no windows. A handful of men had gathered in groups of two and three, but silence fell as I was guided past them to where a pole had been bolted in place at the back of the room.

"Oh, that's the purpose of the outfit, is it? You expect me to do a pole dance for you," I remarked. Who said sarcasm was the lowest form of wit?

    Matthew didn't answer. Instead, he stared straight ahead while unlocking the cuff on his wrist, and then he manoeuvred me around so that he could handcuff me to the pole with my hands behind my back. Once he'd clicked the cuff into place, he moved to face me, making it so that no one else in the room could see his face. "I'm sorry, Emma. I really am," he mouthed. No sound came from his mouth, but a single tear escaped from his left eye.

    As if on cue, his name sounded from the back of the room. "Matthew! Is she ready?"

    "Yes, Father," Matthew replied. His voice sounded steady, but he never took his eyes off me, and in them I saw real and genuine anguish.

    "Good. I have a few things to attend to and then we'll begin, shall we?"

Chapter 18 – Ellie
Monday 3rd June 2019

The dog's growl reverberated around the short corridor. It was only six or eight feet in length, with a door on either side leading into what looked like a pantry on the left and an office on the right. The dog's lip twitched as its growl morphed into a snarl.

Scott froze. "Stay back," he hissed to Ellie, holding out his hand to block her from stepping forwards.

"What is it?"

"A dog," Scott replied, never taking his eyes away from the beast.

"Only a dog?" Ellie asked, easily ducking under his arm. She crouched down low and began talking softly, her eyes firmly fixed on the floor. "Good boy… you're a handsome one, aren't you? What are you? A shepherd? You don't look quite like a shepherd though, not exactly… hmmm… let me think…."

"Ellie, what are you doing?" Scott spoke through gritted teeth, not daring to move.

"Making friends… doggy style." Ellie kept her voice low. She risked a quick glance at the dog. While its muzzle was still fixed into a grimace, it had started to relax, lifting its head slightly and pricking its ears. "Oh, you like that, do you?" Ellie continued talking. "Has no one ever talked nicely to you? I bet they haven't, have they? Mean demons. They're the baddies here, not us. You like us…"

Taking it very slowly, she inched her hand towards her pocket.

"Ellie…"

Ellie ignored Scott and wormed her fingers into her jeans. Just as slowly, she pulled out a meaty treat. "Would you like this?" she asked, offering the treat out towards the dog.

Scott held his breath, but the dog tentatively sniffed the air.

"You would like this," Ellie exclaimed, a smile lighting up her face. Keeping her movements slow and steady, she tossed the treat towards the dog. It landed halfway between her and where the dog was standing, forcing the dog to slink closer if it wanted the treat.

"Ellie…" Scott said again.

"Shush," Ellie hushed. "There's a good boy," she said to the dog. "It's okay, you can have it. It's tasty. Well, all the dogs that come into Cedar's like it. A nice crunchy biscuit, with a beef-flavoured middle. Does that sound good to you?"

It felt like hours passed, but eventually the dog took a small step forward. First one and then another. It took a while, but gradually it crept towards the treat, until it could reach out and snatch it.

"I'm sorry, boy, I haven't got any more," Ellie said when the dog had finished eating, a trace of sorrow in her voice. She took the opportunity to stand, watching the dog carefully for signs of aggression. When it didn't move, she offered her hand out for it to smell. It didn't immediately react, so Ellie was forced to leave her hand hanging for a while until, after several long minutes, it moved. "Good boy," she crooned as the dog sniffed her hand. "Now then, do you know any commands? Do you know 'go to your bed'?" she asked.

The dog gazed up at Ellie, wagging its tail. It was mostly tan in colour, with a black muzzle, black ears, and black eyes that gleamed in the semi-darkness of the house.

"You do know 'go to your bed,' don't you?" Ellie continued. "Go on then, go to your bed," she finished in an authoritative tone.

The dog yipped but did as instructed, rising to its full height and trotting obediently into one of the rooms off the corridor.

Scott was finally able to breathe again. "Ellie," he exclaimed. "How did you do that, and why do you have dog treats in your pocket?"

"Vet nurse," Ellie replied, shrugging her shoulders, as if that answered Scott's question.

The corridor opened out into an industrial-looking kitchen that ran the whole width of the house. Ellie and Scott quickly skirted the stainless-steel island that dominated the space and found themselves at the start of a second corridor, this one much longer. From what they could see there were doors evenly spaced along its length on both the left and the right.

"It looks like a hotel, doesn't it?" Scott whispered, nodding at the walls before tentatively stepping out from the relative safety of the kitchen onto the corridor's beige carpet.

"It does," Ellie followed along behind Scott, "but I've never seen marks like those in a hotel before." She pointed up at the ceiling, where there was a line of strange symbols.

Scott didn't look up; his focus was on what lay ahead. "They must be the runes," he guessed.

"I suppose so," Ellie agreed. Unlike Scott, her eyes were everywhere.

"Can you hear anything?" Scott asked, not turning his head.

"Only my own heart beating. It's racing."

Scott grunted. "Mine too, but if you can't hear anything, hopefully that means we're alone." Scott paused before adding, "I have to say, I'm surprised at how easy it's been so far. First of all, the back door was open... now this corridor is empty... I thought we'd have seen someone by now."

"Do you think it's a trap?" Ellie asked, sweat trickling down her back.

"Or else everyone's busy."

"Let's assume tha—" Ellie started to say before grabbing hold of Scott's arm, stopping him in his tracks. "Scott! Someone's coming."

"Hey!" Someone shouted from behind them before Ellie or Scott had time to move.

Ellie froze. They'd been caught!

"You there. Are you going to the ritual?"

Scott turned, smiling weakly. "Erm, yeah, sure. We're on our way there now." He stumbled over his words.

"Good. You can help me then."

Ellie finally forced her feet to move, even though her legs felt weak. She needed to see who'd spotted them. She needed to see if she'd finally met her first demon. As she turned, she took a deep breath and tensed her body, ready to deal with whatever she saw. Ever since Abaddon had given her the gift of sight, she'd been able to see both of Abaddon's forms: the one she chose to present to the world and her angelic self. At first, the images had flickered between the two, but now Ellie could see both of Abaddon's forms simultaneously. But what would a demon look like? Would she be able to control the nauseating flicker?

The tension drained from Ellie's body as she lifted her chin. Relief flooded her every cell. The man—because it was just a man—who'd interrupted their back and forth was short and stocky, with a full head of black hair and a neatly trimmed beard that had started to go grey. He was standing twenty or thirty feet away from them, in an open doorway, one that had been closed only moments before.

"Of course. What do you need?" Scott answered. Ellie, who knew Scott better than he knew himself, heard the slight tremor in his voice.

"Wait…" The man stepped fully into the corridor and looked sharply at both Ellie and Scott. "Who are you again?" he asked.

"Me?"

"Yes, you." The man's eyes narrowed. "I don't recognise you."

"We've never met. That's why you don't recognise me." Scott shrugged.

"I've met everyone here," the man replied flatly, pulling a gun from behind his back and pointing it squarely at Scott's chest. "Now, tell me… who are you?"

The relief that Ellie had felt only moments previously fled. Demons were one thing, but guns? She knew that she was stronger and faster than most people, but was she that much stronger and faster? And the man held the gun easily—he clearly knew what he was doing.

Time slowed down and silence descended. Ellie heard Scott try and explain away their presence, but she couldn't discern his words. Was he mumbling? Ellie didn't think so, but she couldn't hear him properly. The man—he'd never said his name—flicked the gun to one side, gesturing for her and Scott to follow him, but Ellie didn't know where he wanted to take them. Scott, however, was playing along. He kept on talking, his hands in the air as if he was surrendering, but all of a sudden, he pushed Ellie to one side and reached for one of the knives that he'd made earlier on. Before the man had realised what Scott was up to, Scott threw the knife. As Ellie stumbled and fell, she watched it flip end over end, flying through the air before embedding itself in the man's forehead. Time jumped forwards, and suddenly Scott was by Ellie's side, pulling her into a seated position.

"Come on, Ellie. We have to go."

"We should… erm…" Ellie started to say, but her voice trailed off into silence.

"Come on, Ellie," Scott repeated. "Get up." He lifted her easily, gently standing her on her feet.

"How did you do that?" Ellie asked, shaking her head to clear away the last of the fuzziness. What had just happened? How had Scott reacted so quickly while she'd been in a daze, mesmerised by the sight of a gun? She broke away from him and stepped closer to where the man lay, crouching down to inspect his wound. Blood had pooled underneath his head, forming a halo.

Scott shrugged. "Blacksmith," he said, mimicking the style in which Ellie had chosen to explain away her success with the dog.

"Blacksmith?" Ellie repeated, rising to her full height.

"Yep."

"That doesn't even begin to explain how you've suddenly become an expert knife thrower."

"Who said it was sudden?" Scott replied. "I've been practicing for years. I told you earlier on that I've made knives before now."

"Well yes, but…"

"But what?"

"You managed to hit him in the forehead."

"That was a bit of luck, wasn't it? I was aiming for his stomach. Maybe the symbol that Abaddon had us carve into the knives is more than just a protective symbol. Now come on, we really do need to go." He purposely turned his back and set off walking.

Ellie was quick to catch up, to put some distance between herself and the body.

"Are you okay?" Ellie asked as they emerged into a spacious foyer.

"Why wouldn't I be?" Scott glanced at her, his brow furrowed.

"You've just killed someone."

Scott shrugged. "I've made peace with it already."

"But…"

"Ellie, I know you're worried about having to take a life, and I'm glad that you are because that's part of what makes you you, but honestly, I accepted that I was probably going to have to kill someone even before we came here tonight. If it's a choice between them or us, I choose us."

Ellie sighed quietly, choosing not to answer, deciding that the time wasn't right for a debate about morality. Instead, she drifted further into the foyer. The beige carpet of the corridor gave way to marble flooring, but the runes continued around the top of the wall. To the left, there was a semi-circular set of windows that pushed the foyer out from the house into the grounds, giving it a sense of grandeur, and to the right, there was a magnificent stairwell. The space had been simply decorated, with only a circular pedestal table in front of the windows, on which stood a glass vase filled with black baccara red roses, cranberry-coloured antirrhinums, and burgundy dahlias nestled in among sprigs of baby's breath and strands of myrtle.

"Ellie…" Scott interrupted Ellie's musings. "Have you seen these?"

"Have I seen what?" Ellie asked, turning from the floral display to see what Scott had found.

"That's Blake, isn't it?" Scott asked, pointing at a photograph on the wall.

Ellie stepped closer and peered in the gloom. "They're all Blake," she remarked. There were hundreds of pictures lining the stairway, and all of them featured Blake. "What do you think this means?"

"Honestly," Scott shrugged, "I don't know. But I do think we must be around about the middle of the house, so I vote we start searching for the ruby." He didn't wait for an answer before walking to the nearest door and pulling it open.

"Scott!" Ellie frowned. Scott's behaviour had changed; he seemed more decisive all of a sudden. Perhaps, because they'd come face-to-face with danger and he'd won, he had a little more confidence? "What if someone had been in there?"

"There isn't," Scott answered, disappearing into the room.

Ellie chased after him and found herself in a suite of rooms rather than a single one, the first of which was a formal sitting room. To her right, a pair of wingback leather chairs faced a floor-to-ceiling stone hearth, and opposite was a huge picture window. Scott, however, was nowhere to be seen. "Scott?" she called, trying to keep her voice down while also raising it. "Where are you?"

"In here," he replied. "I think I've found something."

Ellie followed the sound of his voice and found herself in a small square nook that was just off the formal sitting room. With the exception of the never-ending runes, the walls were undecorated and the floor was plainly flagged.

"Scott!" Ellie gasped, stopping dead. In the centre of the nook was an intricately carved circular table, inlaid with rubies. Twelve individual jewels had been sunk into the wooden top of the table until they were each flush with the surface, placed so as to effectively form the face of a clock.

"Do you think we need to shatter each one?"

"I guess… I don't know…" Ellie started to answer Scott's question, but then paused, frowning.

"What?" Scott glanced up at Ellie.

"It's just…" Ellie cocked her head to one side. "Well, you said it earlier on. Don't you think this has all been a little too easy? If the rubies are so important, wouldn't you have hidden them?"

"I don't know, maybe."

"I know I would have. If it's the rubies that are powering the runes, then I'd have them under lock and key."

"Ah, but because of the runes, the demons know that the angels can't get in here."

"What about everyone else?"

"Who else do they need protecting from?"

"Us."

"Well, yes, but they don't know about us."

"Don't they?"

"Of course not."

Ellie shook her head. "I just… I don't know. I have a bad feeling about all of this."

"I get that. It's been a stressful time, and it's been traumatic getting here. We were almost caught in the gardens, that mongrel dog nearly ripped my face off—"

"It did not!"

"And then, well…." Scott's voice trailed off.

Ellie huffed. "I know, I hear what you're saying, but this, it's just… too obvious."

"Abaddon said that we needed to destroy the ruby, and we've found the ruby—several actually—just like she said we would."

"I know what she said." Ellie started pacing. "I trust Abaddon, I do. I believe that what she told us, she told us in good faith. Hell, she's probably dying for us to succeed so that she can get in here and start another war with the demons. But, in all honesty, how could she possibly know about the ruby?"

"I'm sure it's just standard rune magic."

"I don't think so. And even if it was once upon a time, I think the demons would have changed their habits by now."

"I don't think demons have it in them to change. That's the point."

"No, I'm sorry, Scott. This has been too easy. We're missing some—" Ellie paused. "Did you hear that?"

"Did I hear what?"

"The door? I just heard the door lock." Ellie darted into the formal sitting room. She'd definitely left the door open, but now it was closed. "Hey!" Ellie shouted, trying the handle. Much to her disgust, the door had indeed been locked.

"Ms. Chapman-Bell, I assume," a voice sounded from out in the corridor. "It's a pleasure to meet you. And might I add that I'm impressed with how insightful you've just been. Of course that does mean that you'll need to be restrained for the foreseeable future."

"Let me out of here!"

"Come now, child, you don't really think that your demands will be met, do you?"

"I…" Ellie didn't know what to say.

"Now then, do make yourself at home in there, won't you?" The voice on the other side of the door sounded sickeningly cheerful. "I've got things to attend to. Oh! And I wouldn't bother trying to escape. I know all about your… ah… shall we say, enhancements. Every door in this house is lined with steel, and the windows are all bulletproof."

"Wait! How…?"

"How did I know about your enhancements? Or how did I know that you were here?" The voice chuckled. "It isn't just Emma that we watch, you know. And as to how I knew you were here: we've had eyes on you ever since you hopped over our wall. If Mr. Thompson had bothered to read his messages, he'd have known that my orders were to leave you and that ogre you're with well alone. My instructions were quite clear."

"But why?"

"Why leave you alone? Ah yes, that's a good question. Let's just say that I was curious. I wanted to know what you'd do. You see, I don't very often get the chance to interact with angels, and even though you're not exactly an angel, I'd hoped that by watching you, I'd gather some new intel. Disappointing, I must say. The ogre was far more entertaining than you. You're nothing more than a scared child. Him, on the other hand... Well, let me just say that that was a very nice throw. Please do pass on my compliments."

"But..."

"But what, my dear? Haven't I covered everything? Oh, I see! You're wondering why I haven't just killed you. I could have done that, of course I could have done, but when the King of Hell is released, I expect he'll be hungry. I'm not sure if Emma on her own will satisfy him. Now then, ta-ta for now. That's what all the kids say, isn't it?"

Ellie distinctly heard the sound of a titter before it went quiet. She turned back towards Scott. "Did you get all of that?" she said before bursting into tears.

"I did," he replied, and then closed the distance between them and took Ellie in his arms. "It's okay," he reassured. "We'll find a way out of this."

"How?" Ellie sobbed.

"I don't know, but I don't intend on becoming demon food, and I'm not letting that happen to you or Emma either. Let's explore the rest of these rooms and see if we can find anything useful."

Ellie nodded into Scott's chest. "Just in case anything does happen to us, I'm sorry, and I—"

"No." Scott let his arms drop and stepped back from Ellie. "We're not going there. Come on, start searching." He turned away, but Ellie suspected that he too had started to cry.

"—love you," Ellie finished quietly.

Ellie and Scott frantically searched the rooms that they'd been locked in, and all the while Ellie berated herself for being so stupid. Why hadn't the thought occurred that she might be leading Scott into a trap? They were going to die, and it was all her fault. Maybe her mum had been right; maybe she should have just killed Emma. She could have done it painlessly, maybe with the drug that her mum had been going to use. But no! She couldn't, she just couldn't.

"Ellie," Scott said eventually, breaking the silence. His voice was tinged with excitement despite the circumstances. "I can hear you worrying from over here."

"No, you can't," Ellie scoffed despite the fear and anxiety that was busy nesting in her body.

"Maybe not literally, but if you chew your fingernails anymore, you'll only have stumps left."

"Very funny," Ellie remarked, unconsciously hiding her hands behind her back.

"Anyway…" Scott drawled. "I think I might have found something." He was standing, staring at the runes.

"Really?" Ellie asked, following his gaze. She didn't see anything; nothing new anyway.

"Have you noticed how all of the runes are linked?"

"What do you mean, 'all linked'?"

"Look," Scott nodded in the same direction that he stared, "the runes… they all have a topper and a tail so that they're touching the one on either side, the line is very thin, but it's there."

"So?"

"So… I think it means there isn't a master. Which means that if we destroy one, we destroy them all."

"But what about the rubies?"

"These rubies?" Scott held out his hand.

"Scott!" Ellie gasped, taking one of the gems from him and holding it up to her eye. The moonlight made it sparkle brightly, casting streaks of red light around the room.

"They popped out of the table easily enough. I don't think they're the power source. I don't know if there's another ruby knocking about, but I've been thinking about what you said. I don't think the rubies are important at all."

"If the rubies aren't important, then what's keeping the runes active?"

"I don't know, but seeing as they're used by demons, I wonder if you're the key to nullifying them."

"Me?"

"Yes, you. Well, your blood. I mean, it's a long shot, but…"

Ellie glanced at Scott, frowning. "Why not your blood?"

"Because you have angel blood in your veins, dummy. I'm just a regular Joe. And we know that your blood is powerful because when you nicked your finger on Blake's blade, Abaddon knew about it."

"But Abaddon said that we needed an iron blade. That's why she had you make one."

"She did indeed, because iron disrupts magic. So, if we smear some of your blood onto one of the blades that Abaddon had me make and stab it into one of the runes…"

"Do you really think it will work?"

"We won't know until we try." Scott smiled.

"What are we waiting for then?" Ellie absentmindedly pocketed the ruby that she'd taken from Scott and held her hand out.

Chapter 19 – Emma
Monday 3rd June 2019 / Tuesday 4th June 2019

The chamber had slowly filled up around me. Where there had only been a handful of men, there were now forty or fifty, but none had spoken to me. Ever since Matthew had handcuffed me to the pole, I'd been ignored, left to my own devices. I'd tried pulling my wrists free, but the cold bite of steel had been unrelenting, and in the end, exhaustion had stilled my struggles. The fact that every single muscle in my body hurt was now a minor inconvenience because what was really bothering me was the white-hot spark of pain that shot through my shoulder blades every so often.

With nothing else to do except cry, I started a visual inspection of my surroundings and the men who'd come to witness the end of the world… just in case. I mean, I knew that it was unlikely I'd live to see another day, but if by some miracle I did survive, I wanted to be able to hunt the bastards down and kill them all. Well, I wanted Blake to do the actual slaying because I wasn't really cut out for such activities and he'd already proven himself to be capable in that department, but still….

I couldn't help but do a mental compare and contrast between Ellie's dream and my own reality. She hadn't exactly dreamt up my future, but she'd come close. Perhaps when Abaddon had made it so that she could *see*, she'd also given her the gift of prophecy, not that I'd ever find out for sure, not unless that miracle did happen.

I'd been stashed towards the back of the room, over on one side. To my left, but set slightly back from where I was standing, there was something akin to an altar, and beyond that a strange symbol had been painted onto the stone floor. Effectively, the pole that I was handcuffed to formed one point of a triangle. Idly I wondered if that meant something specific or if the setup was purely aesthetic.

The altar, if that's what it was, was the only source of light at my end of the room. Some kind of table had been covered with a dark cloth, on which stood six matte black candles, arranged in two groups of three, one at either end of the table. In between them, an upside-down cross gleamed in the weak light.

The symbol that had been painted on the floor looked like a star with seven points, although the points weren't evenly spaced out. Cutting through the middle of the star, there was another upside-down cross. Clearly upside-down crosses meant something to these guys. A circle had been drawn around both the star and the cross so that the points of the star and the ends of the cross touched its circumference.

After staring at the symbol for a while, I let my eyes roam. All of the men (and I wasn't being sexist here, they were all men) were dressed exactly alike, in the same black suit that Matthew was wearing. Most were older, but several were around about Matthew's age. Perhaps they were the others like him, the ones who'd had their lives dictated by my choices.

What brought you all here, I wondered. Why would anyone side with demons? Had everyone in the room been told the same lies as Matthew, or did some of them know the truth? I had so many questions, but before I could lose myself in my own mind, a voice sounded immediately on my left, bringing me back to reality.

"Brothers! Sons! Welcome all on this, the most auspicious day of all time." It was Terrance speaking; I recognised his voice.

So, you're Matthew's father, are you? I remarked rhetorically to myself. I'd never actually got a good look of him before. He was about Matthew's height, but he was bulkier around the middle. Matthew had a swimmer's body, whereas Terrance looked more like a weightlifter. The face was much the same though, but Matthew's was kinder somehow. Terrance looked like he'd swallowed a wasp.

Terrance paused momentarily before turning to face me. "Emma, we've waited patiently throughout the centuries for you to come." He smiled, but if he was trying to put me at ease, he failed. "Your help with the ritual is much appreciated, and you never know… you might yet live. The King of Hell might choose you for a bride instead of his first meal."

"Fuck you!" I muttered. I rarely swore, but I figured that if ever I was justified in using the f-word, it was now.

"Now, now, my child. There's no need for that kind of talk in here. We are in a sacred space after all."

"Sacred?"

Hush now. Don't play his games, Johnna interjected, causing a nub of shame to wash over me.

"Now then, where was I?" Terrance was clearly a showman. He paused, a slight frown on his face. "Ah yes." He clapped his hands together. "The King of Hell might yet choose the Guardian and her ape-like suitor for his first meal."

"Ellie!" I gasped.

Oh good, she's here, Johnna commented.

Good? It's not good. I don't want her to die as well.

I've been telling you all along that it's up to Ellie. If she wasn't here, how could she play her part?

But… but… who's her suitor, do you think?

I assume he's referring to your brother. Now—

Scott! The thought hadn't occurred that Ellie's 'ape-like' suitor would be Scott. Of course, I knew they were in love, but he didn't have any of Ellie's gifts, nor was he obligated like Ellie was. Why had he put himself in danger by following her here?

—be quiet, we need to listen.

Terrance had continued talking while Johnna and I had had our quick conversation, "…Him here. Brothers! Sons! It is time for us to amend the runes… Do it!" he snapped, pointing towards the back of the room.

I turned my head so that I could look where Terrance had pointed. At the back of the room, four of the 'men' shimmered and changed into beings that were most definitely not men. My mouth went very dry in an instant. The men—the demons—stood head and shoulders above everyone else, their skin a dull black colour. And their eyes… there was no pupil or coloured iris, instead the whole thing was a solid block of dark maroon.

"Do it!" Terrance barked for a second time.

As one, when Terrance commanded it, the demons spread their wings out wide, stretching them up towards the ceiling. I hadn't even realised that demons would have wings, but there they were. Each one had five 'ribs,' ending in a hooked talon. Between the ribs, a leathery looking skin-like material was stretched taught. It was an oily colour, almost a pearlescent form of black, swirled with reds and blues. The wings of each demon had a slightly different blend of red and blue proving that each demon was unique, its own being as it were, but nevertheless they acted as one. Using the talons of their wings, each of the four demons scored through a different rune, acting in perfect synchronicity.

And just like that, I could feel Blake again. His emotions were like a wave washing over me. In an instant I could feel his pain. I'd suffered, of course I had, but at least I'd always known what had been happening to me. Blake's suffering had been immeasurably worse. The not knowing had been an exquisite kind of mental torture for him.

"Blake," I gasped. How was that possible? He had to be close by for our emotions to collide. Perhaps he'd always been close by. I *had* connected with him the other day after all, but how had he found me? I very much doubted that Seith had been able to follow my trail. Surely as soon as I'd been packed into the back of Matthew's car, my scent had stopped dead. And while I had the utmost respect for the police, there was nothing to connect me with my kidnappers, so there was no way for them to trace my whereabouts.

Do not let him come here! Johnna snapped. *Not yet anyway.*

Blake? I whispered, but not out loud. *If you can hear me, please don't come here. It will be much worse for you than it is for me. Please, stay away. Run! Go to the other side of the world and don't ever look back.*

Blake didn't reply, but a flicker of emotion rippled across my skin. It was hope. He might not have heard me, but he'd felt my emotions in the same way that I'd felt his.

Terrance was enjoying the theatrics. Although he couldn't possibly know about my private conversations, he hadn't missed the sheen of sweat that had coated my forehead, or the way in which my shoulders had sagged. He took a step in my direction. "Oh dear," he crooned, "have you not seen a demon before? Aren't they magnificent?"

I couldn't help myself from replying. "I imagine that angels are nicer to look at."

"Angels!" Terrance spat, his body becoming rigid. "Angels are despicable beings. They would rather the portal remains closed to ensure the safety of all humanity. They care nothing about the power that I—" Terrance stopped abruptly, clamping his jaw shut. Clearly he'd said too much.

Quickly I scanned the crowd, looking to see if anyone reacted to Terrance's words. Everyone remained enthralled. Everyone except Matthew. The colour drained from his face, and he took a step forward, only to be stopped by an older man who was standing next to him.

Terrance didn't seem to notice; he was too busy brushing non-existent flecks of dust from his suit.

"Now then, where were we?" he continued talking as though nothing untoward had happened. "Ah yes… you," he glanced at me, "need to call **him** here."

"Never!"

Terrance chuckled. "We'll see about that, shall we?" He pulled a knife from behind his back and walked towards me. The smile never left his face as he traced the blade from my ear, along the line of my chin, and down my neck towards my bust. I didn't even realise he'd sliced into my skin until I felt the blood dribble down towards my cleavage. And then the pain hit.

Blake, do not come here! I commanded. "You'll have to try harder than that," I scoffed through gritted teeth despite the fire that danced along my nerve endings.

"Daaarling, that was only a precursor to what I have planned for you."

"Father! Stop!" Matthew shouted from the crowd.

Terrance whipped his head around and glared at his son. "How dare you interrupt me?" His eyes, no longer focussed on me, were like lasers boring a hole in rock.

"I only meant… it's just that… I thought time was of the essence." Matthew stumbled over his words.

"Did you now?" Terrance purred, his voice dangerously low. "That's what you thought, was it?" he remarked, his eyebrows raised. "Somehow I don't believe you." His face turned blank. "You've always been too much of a baby for our line of work. I should have thrown you out years ago, but no… I trusted you with the most important job of all. I let you get close to her, to the one, the Key. I gave you a chance to prove yourself and this… this is how you repay me?" Terrance paused, seemingly gathering his thoughts. "You insolent little cretin." He shook his head. "I should feed you to the demons…" Matthew blanched. "I should… no, wait… I know what I should do… a wet wuss like you. I should make you force Emma to call **him** here. How would you like that, son? You can have the ultimate honour. Come on, come here." He beckoned for Matthew to join him.

Matthew didn't move until he was pushed forwards by others. I held my breath, not knowing what was going to happen next. Terrance forced the blade into Matthew's hand. "You will either make Emma suffer so she calls for her beloved, or else I will peel layers of skin from your body until you collapse in agony. And I will enjoy every minute of it. It's your choice."

Matthew paled and took a tighter hold of the knife.

Be strong, Emma, Johnna whispered.

That's easy for you to say, I muttered, watching Matthew toy with the knife that he now gripped in his hand.

Matthew turned away from his father to look at me. His eyes were wide with terror and sweat beaded his forehead. He took a tentative step in my direction before glancing back at his father.

"It's your choice, boy," Terrance reiterated.

"I'm sorry, Emma." Matthew spoke directly to me, his voice barely audible. "It will be worse for you if he does it. I'm doing you a favour, don't you see?"

The room seemed to disappear as I watched Matthew inch his way towards me, all the while reassuring himself that what he was doing was for the best. To be fair to him, he probably had a point. Whatever Terrance had planned would be much worse than whatever Matthew could come up with. Terrance was a sadist. There was no other way to describe him. He revelled in inflicting pain on others. Matthew at least seemed to care.

Without hesitation, when he was close enough, Matthew thrust the knife into my stomach, and all of my other aches and pains vanished as the blade sliced through muscle before connecting with one of my internal organs. Which one, I didn't know. Once upon a time, I'd been good at human biology, but rational thought had left the building.

Pure agony encapsulated me in a little bubble. I sank into the depths of despair; I drowned in the sea of oblivion. And then Blake was at my side, gently caressing my cheek. I'd meant to keep him away, to suffer whatever was coming without pulling him to me, but there he was. Unconsciously I'd forced him through space to be by my side.

"Emma." He breathed in my scent.

"You need to leave," I mumbled. Why was it so hard to speak? Where had all of my energy gone?

"I'm not leaving without you," Blake declared.

I didn't have time to answer before Terrance interrupted our reunion. "Now!" he commanded.

He does like to bark his orders, I thought to myself, winning the random-thought-of-the-day competition.

We need to get you out of here, Blake answered, even though I hadn't been talking to him. His eyes had still not left mine. He hadn't seemed to notice that he was in a room full of people, or that he was in quite a lot of danger.

"Do it!" Terrance continued to boss people around. But before anyone could do anything, the whole building shook.

Because I was still secured to the pole, I wasn't able to steady myself as I swung to the left before slowly slumping forwards, the knife still firmly embedded in my stomach. My knees gave way as Blake stumbled, almost head-butting the pole, and of course I couldn't do anything to help him out either. He ended up on the floor with me. Both Terrance and Matthew were thrown to one side, although both managed to stay on their feet, and the crowd of men surged forwards like an ocean full of rage. Even the demons, who were still at the back of the room, couldn't keep both of their feet securely planted on the floor.

What's happening? I asked Blake. *Is it an earthquake?* I'd never been in an earthquake before, but what else could up-end a whole building?

I don't know. I think it's Ellie. I think she's found the ruby.

Ellie? I asked, more than a little confused. *What ruby?*

Murmurs of unease rippled through the crowd. Odd words reached my ears even though I wasn't really listening to the men… explosion… runes… angels…

What do they mean?

It's not important right now. All that matters is that we get you out of here.

But Blake, I'm— I was going to explain that I was handcuffed to a pole and most likely dying. I knew what a knife in the stomach meant. I wasn't bleeding out because Matthew had left the blade firmly embedded inside of me, but I assumed I was bleeding internally. At least I'd gotten to see Blake again, to be enveloped in his love for me while my life slipped from me. But I didn't get the chance to say any of that before Terrance, dictator that he was, demanded that his men 'start the chant.' He had to repeat himself, but eventually the men who were gathered started speaking in a peculiar language. They were quiet at first, hesitant almost, but eventually their 'song' grew, swelling as they became more confident.

It's the language of demons, Johnna remarked, not that I'd asked.

You need to be ready, Emma, she continued.

Ready for what?

You'll see, she answered.

The chanting continued. At first nothing happened, well, nothing that I could see anyway. But the colour slowly drained from Blake's face. All of a sudden, he scrambled away from me, not that he made it very far before he collapsed onto the floor.

"Blake!" I screamed, desperately trying to free my wrists once more.

"Keep going!" Terrance paused his own chanting to demand more from his entourage.

The chanting continued. It had a hypnotic rise and fall that lulled me. I stopped struggling and started to listen. If only I could puzzle out what the words meant, I felt like I'd understand everything.

Ignore it, Emma. Focus on Blake. Johnna brought me back to myself.

I'd never really understood what it meant for someone to writhe in agony, but that's exactly what Blake did. His back arched upwards so that only his hips and shoulders were on the floor. His hands and feet curled in on themselves. He seemed unable to move at will, unable to fight the attack that he was under.

"Blake," I sobbed, tears welling up in my eyes, but Blake didn't—or perhaps couldn't—respond. As I watched, his suffering continued. Somehow his body seemed to tear. A split formed in his very being. It started near his clavicle, ran diagonally across his body, and ended at the top of his thigh. A black glossy light bled from the 'wound.' Of course, it wasn't exactly a wound. No one had touched Blake; he hadn't been cut, not like me. His body was simply being torn apart by unseen forces. And he was clearly in a lot of pain. His body was drenched in sweat, his jaw was tightly clenched together, his brow was furrowed, and he cried out more than once.

Emma, you need to get ready to act, Johnna advised.

I still don't understand what you mean by 'act'? I replied, watching the split in Blake's abdomen grow wider as the chanting continued. A clawed hand started to emerge from out of his body, making me feel sick. The pain that had seeped into every single one of my joints was forgotten, but I tasted vomit at the back of my throat.

Now, Emma! Close the portal.

What do you mean, close the portal? I don't know how to close the portal.

Emma, you have all the power that you need; you're the Key. You can control everything he does.

I can't! I don't know how.

Yes, you do. You've done it before. You can do it again.

I haven't... I don't...

Johnna didn't answer, but images flickered in my mind, images of Blake exorcising Anais. Johnna was reminding me that I had, in fact, forced Blake to do as I'd demanded once before. I'd promised him I'd never do it again, but...

Blake, I shouted, *close the portal!*

Nnargh, Blake muttered while Johnna tsked.

Emma, she barked, sounding a lot like Terrance, *you need to really mean it.*

I took a deep breath in, trying to centre myself, trying to push past everything that was happening, and as I exhaled, I built a picture in my mind. I saw a pair of solid dark wooden doors trimmed with iron that needed to be slammed shut. On my side of the doors, the sky was blue and the sun was shining down from above, but on the other side, a storm was raging. Black clouds roiled overhead, forked lightning repeatedly struck the ground, and rain fell in sheets.

Blake. Close. The. Portal! I commanded, imagining the doors closing. They were huge, and they were heavy. I had to push against them with every ounce of strength that I could muster, but slowly they started coming together.

Blake whimpered. Somehow the tear was still growing wider, and the clawed hand continued to reach upwards, out from Blake's body.

It's not working, I cried, panic tightening a noose around my neck. Time was running out. Terrance and his band of merry men were winning. The portal was still opening. And they had all the time in the world. They weren't dying.

Use the power of your ancestors, Johnna snapped. Faces flashed before my eyes. Johnna's... my nan's... all of the women who had ever carried the soul before me. And suddenly I knew that I would succeed because I wasn't alone. In fact, I'd never been alone. It wasn't just me fighting this battle, I had a family, and together, we were the Key.

Keeping the image of my ancestors in my mind, I sat up

straighter—still handcuffed to the pole and still with a knife embedded in my gut, but now I felt in control. The pain and fear from earlier on evaporated as I squared my shoulders, letting my spine drop into its natural s-shape. I breathed in again, but this time, as I exhaled, I didn't just build a picture in my mind, I built a whole world. And I didn't just watch it form, I stepped inside of it. I stood alongside my ancestors, and together we pushed the door closed. As one, we commanded Blake to do our bidding. Our voices rang out in the chamber, drowning out the demonic chanting, and Blake was forced to hear us.

The tear that had formed in Blake's body was mended in much the same way that a zip pulls together two pieces of fabric. The demon that had been forcing his way into our world snatched his hand back at the very last second, and Terrance howled out his frustration.

For a single second, an unexpected hush fell on the chamber, and I had a moment, just a moment mind you, to see that Blake was going to survive his ordeal before chaos erupted.

"What the fuck have you done?" Terrance snarled at me. "You need to undo it right now." He continued ranting obscenities, but I zoned out. I looked past him because fighting had broken out at the back of the chamber. Angels had appeared from somewhere. I smiled; I couldn't help myself. I forgot that I was still a captive, still locked in place with a knife in my stomach, still at the mercy of a madman, and Blake was not yet in a position to rescue me. "You... this is all your fault..." I tuned back in to what Terrance was saying. "I'll see you in Hell for this." Terrance closed the gap between us, grabbed my hair, and smacked my head against the pole. It didn't take long for darkness to descend, but as my vision wavered, I saw Blake rising to his full height, scythe in hand.

Chapter 20 – Blake
Tuesday 4th June 2019

"Seith," Blake called, reaching into the ether to retrieve his weapon, his strength slowly returning. Fury gnawed at his innards. He'd been consumed by anger in the past, but before it had always been for selfish reasons. He'd been jealous of others, and lonely because of the nature of his existence. He'd wanted something that he couldn't have, and irritation had wormed its way into his psyche and threaded itself around his soul. His soul had then acted like an echo chamber, amplifying the irritation until it had grown into a white-hot rage that, over time, had settled into an ice-cold fury. But now his anger had taken on a new dimension because it wasn't driven by jealousy or loneliness. For the first time in his life, it was driven by love. Of course, he'd been angry when Peter had threatened Emma's life, but he'd still been confused about his feelings for her then. Now, he was well aware that what he felt for Emma was love, and the fact that she'd been hurt was making him apoplectic with rage.

Seith appeared in an instant, hackles already raised, and Terrance's men fell like blades of grass in his wake. As one, they withdrew from the snarling beast, but at their backsides there were angels, and the angels were not merciful.

Blake took a step towards Terrance, already swinging his scythe. Terrance would pay for committing the ultimate crime, just as Peter had paid. At least Peter hadn't been the monster that Terrance was—he hadn't tortured Emma, he hadn't hurt her for his own gain. He'd been fixated with her, yes, but his soul wasn't black. Even so, Blake had had no qualms about ordering his execution; he certainly felt none about ending Terrance's life. As his scythe sliced through skin and bone with the ease of a hot knife sliding through butter, his only thought was of Emma. His innate ability to sense death told him that her life was draining away; she had only moments to live, and there was nothing he could do to prevent her death. But curiously, all he felt from her was love. She was content, all of her fear and anguish had drained away when *she'd* saved *him*.

Terrance's head and the upper part of his torso fell to the left, while his legs crumpled where he'd been standing. Blood pooled around both of the body parts, but his soul remained standing. Even in death, he held himself arrogantly, fanning the flames of Blake's anger. Blake wasted no time, swinging his scythe for a second time. It whistled through the air, through Terrance's soul, which exploded into a cloud of jet-black particles that hung suspended in the air for a moment before dissipating into nothing.

Blake couldn't help but watch Terrance's life unfold before his eyes. He'd been malevolent even as a child, delighting in the torture of others. He'd been young when he'd made his first sacrifice, taking advice from his father on the best way to slit a throat. And he'd enjoyed it. In fact, he'd delighted in it, going so far as to smear the blood of his victim across his own forehead, letting it run down his face and into his mouth so that he could taste it. In that moment, any sense of humanity that he'd been born with had been crushed, snuffed out by an overwhelming desire to bathe in the blood of his enemies. A true psychopath had been born that day.

As an adult, Terrance had learned all about his father's organisation. He'd learned that angels and demons were real, that they were trapped on Earth because the portal had been slammed shut. He'd learned that if he wanted more power, he'd need to open the portal, he'd need to welcome more demons into the world. But to do that, he'd need the Key to meet 'him,' not that anyone ever said who 'he' was.

While Terrance was still a young man, he'd watched over Emma's grandmother, Betty. On more than one occasion, he'd chatted with her thinking that if he could make her his own, he'd be able to control her, but each time he'd invited her out, she'd politely refused him. Perhaps she'd sensed the darkness that marred his soul? Obviously Terrance didn't know why she'd snubbed him, but it made him more determined to destroy her or, at the very least, one of her descendants.

Despite everything that he knew, Terrance had never once heard the phrase 'Keeper of Souls.' Blake couldn't help but think that in another time, in another place, if he'd have reaped Terrance's soul out of context, he'd have assumed he was a madman, a psychopath who suffered from hallucinations.

While Terrance's life played through in Blake's mind eye, Blake dropped to his knees by Emma's side, abandoning his scythe to the ether, trusting Seith to guard his back. She was still breathing, but she'd wilted. Her head was slumped forwards, lolling on one side, and her chin was resting on her chest.

"Emma... my love." Blake reached up and brushed her hair from her face. "Don't leave me. I can't live without you." Tears welled up in his eyes, quickly overflowing and streaming down his cheeks. "Don't make me reap your soul. I can't. It'll kill me."

Emma didn't answer, but Blake felt her love for him pulse in his abdomen.

"Blake!" Abaddon interrupted. When she'd arrived, Blake didn't know. His world had collapsed in on itself; all that mattered was Emma. Even the sound of the ongoing battle behind him was being drowned out by the sound of Emma's breathing. "Blake!" Abaddon snapped again. "You need to get out of here."

"I can't leave her," Blake mumbled.

"Take her with you then."

"I can't." Blake didn't look up; his head was bowed low with grief. Never before had he felt so inept. His soulmate's life was draining away in front of his eyes, and there was nothing he could do about it. He couldn't even take her from the chamber in which she'd been tortured; he didn't have the power to move her so that she could at least die in peace. *He* could go wherever he wanted, but he couldn't take Emma with him. *He* could move between places because he was mostly a spirit, but Emma was flesh and blood; she was bound in place by the laws of physics.

"Oh for heaven's sake!" Abaddon muttered. "This might hurt a little bit," she said before glancing over her shoulder at Seith. "And you, it's up to you if you follow along or not. I don't care either way." With that, she took hold of Blake's shoulder with her left hand and Emma's with her right.

Blake barely had time to register the shock of being touched by an angel, by Abaddon, before he was back in Ellie's apartment.

"Emma! Blake!" Ellie and Scott exclaimed at the same time. They were standing in the kitchen, but Blake barely saw them. Only Emma mattered now.

"Seith!" Ellie added. "Oh my God, you're all alive? How? What happened?"

Abaddon took a moment to make sure that Emma was laid down on the sofa, and then she stared at Ellie and Scott before turning to Blake. "I'm sorry, Blake. I really am, but perhaps it's for the best."

"For the best?" Ellie repeated, pushing past Scott so she could look at Emma.

Blake barely registered her gasp. As soon as Abaddon had released her hold on him, he'd collapsed on the floor, his legs simply folding in on themselves, and then he'd scooted closer to Emma so that he could stroke her hair, just like he had all of those months before when he'd first reached out and touched her. At the time, he'd thought hers was the softest hair in all the world, and he still believed it now.

Out of the corner of his eye, he saw Ellie take a step backwards, her hands covering her mouth. "No," she cried, tears filling her icy blue eyes. As she stepped backwards, Scott pulled her into him, wrapping his arms around her. His face had turned a curious mottled colour.

"I need to get back to my brothers and sisters," Abaddon announced. "They need me too." But if anyone replied, Blake didn't hear them. He was vaguely aware that Seith had rested his front paws on the back of the sofa and was also watching over Emma, but Emma was Blake's only concern. He didn't dare take his eyes off her, she was his everything, but soon, she would be nothing. She'd be reduced to flesh and bone. Her life would be over.

The only sound that Blake could hear was Emma's breathing; everything else disappeared as a hush blanketed the room. It was slowing down. It wouldn't be long until she was gone. One… two… three… and then… that was it.

Blake's heart shattered into a million pieces when Emma took her last breath, but his mind refused to accept what had happened. He was too stunned to cry out despite the pain of grief. It couldn't possibly true. She couldn't be dead. She'd survived so much, it wasn't fair. Even though he'd known it was coming, he couldn't accept it. Gently, he reached up and smoothed out Emma's hair before standing to attend to her some more. He placed her hands together, loosely draping them over her stomach, and he straightened her legs so that they were no longer resting where they'd fallen. He tugged at the meagre clothing that she'd been forced to wear, wanting it to cover what it could, and then he wrenched the knife from her stomach, absently abandoning it behind him. By the time he was finished, he was able to convince himself that

Emma was only sleeping. Nothing else made sense anyway, except... he couldn't quite reconcile the idea of Emma sleeping with the fact that she had a hole punctured in her stomach. Her skin had taken on a ghastly pallor and blood had dried along her jawline. Gravity had done what gravity does, and it had trickled down the side of her neck before drying. Bruises covered her arms, evidence that she'd been manhandled, and there were bluish-grey bags underneath her eyes. But she was only sleeping. That was the only explanation that Blake could accept.

    Satisfied, he leant to kiss her, wanting only to feel her lips on his, but the Keeper of Souls was forced to act. And while he reaped Emma's soul, Seith howled and both Ellie and Scott cried.

Chapter 21 – Ellie
Tuesday 4th June 2019

The relief of having Emma safely home had been a brief moment of pure unadulterated pleasure. For a split second, Ellie had really believed they'd done it—they'd somehow won! And not only that, they'd all survived. It was incredible. And it was *literally* incredible because it wasn't true. They hadn't all survived. Emma was gone; she'd paid the ultimate price. Ellie had been prepared for someone to die, just not Emma. They were supposed to be saving Emma, so how could she be dead? What could possibly have gone wrong?

She and Scott had managed to get into the demon house easily enough; in fact, it had been a little too easy. Of course she now knew that was because it had been a trap. But despite that, despite the fact that Abaddon had sent them in to search for a ruby, assuring them that only a ruby could be powering the runes keeping her and Blake out, they'd done what they went in to do. Naturally a ruby had had nothing to do with it.

Scott had been the one who'd worked out that all of the runes were linked and that she would be able to disrupt their power—well, her blood would anyway. Naturally, she'd readily offered out her hand to Scott, who'd been as gentle as possible when he'd sliced through her skin, but you can only be so gentle if you want to make someone bleed. He'd dragged the blade of one of his knives across the palm of her hand until it was coated in her blood, and then, after changing his grip on the handle, he'd rammed it as hard as he could into one of the runes.

After that, chaos had ensued.

First of all, the runes themselves had appeared to shimmer. Each one in turn, starting with the one that had been struck, had briefly turned from red to blue. The effect had danced around the room, and although Ellie hadn't been able to see out into the corridor, she'd assumed it had rippled across the whole of the rune network. And then, all at once, every single rune had exploded outwards.

Scott had snatched his knife back, before wrapping his arms

around her body and turning them both away from the wall, shielding her from flying debris. The whole house had trembled from the shock of hundreds, if not thousands, of mini detonations, and consequently, plasterboard flew in all directions while furniture and ornaments wobbled, teetered, and, in some cases, fell.

An ornately decorated vase had been one of the casualties in the room where Ellie and Scott had been trapped. As the house had begun to shake, it'd rocked back and forth on the mantelpiece before gravity had taken hold and it had fallen to the floor, whereupon it had shattered into a million pieces, scattering small pieces of gold pot across the floor.

"We need to get out of here," Ellie had yelled at Scott.

"And go where?" Scott had yelled back.

But before Ellie could answer, Abaddon had appeared, taken both of their hands, and transported them back to Ellie's apartment. Just like that, they'd moved through space, going from the demon house to Ellie's comfortable little kitchen in an instant. Abaddon had only stayed long enough to heal Ellie's hand before excitedly exclaiming that she needed to get back.

Ellie had barely had time to absorb the fact that she and Scott were still alive when Abaddon had appeared again, this time with Blake and Emma in tow, and Seith following along behind.

Ellie's heart had jumped into her throat, singing in delight. Not only had they saved Emma, they'd somehow stopped the apocalypse! For just a second, she'd been overjoyed, and then Abaddon had said, "I'm sorry, Blake. I really am, but perhaps it's for the best."

"For the best?" Ellie had asked, pushing past Scott to see what Abaddon meant. "No!" she'd exclaimed. And now Emma was dead; not only dead, but Blake was reaping her soul.

Ellie watched, unable to tear her eyes away as Blake laid the briefest of kisses on Emma's lips. *Please, Emma, please wake up,* she prayed, hoping that Emma would wrap her arms around Blake's neck before tugging him into her. In her mind's eye, she could see Emma laughing as Blake overbalanced. But even in life, that wasn't Emma. She wasn't known for practical jokes; she wasn't even a laugh-out-loud kind of person. She was a serious soul. She was loyal to those that she loved, but hers was a trust that had to be earned.

Tears fell unchecked from Ellie's eyes, and a hiccupping sob escaped her body. Scott murmured something in her ear, but she couldn't discern the words. Something about it being all right, but how was it ever going to be all right again? Her best friend was dead. Not only that, but she'd suffered horribly if the state of her body was anything to go by.

Blake—the Keeper of Souls—wasted no time in fulfilling his duties. As Ellie understood it, for him, reaping a soul was second nature. He couldn't not reap a soul, but couldn't he have waited a few minutes? Couldn't he have given them time to grieve? Or perhaps try mouth-to-mouth? Ellie was a vet nurse after all, maybe she could have saved Emma? But no, it was too late for that because Blake was already administering the Kiss of Death, and Ellie could clearly see that he was breathing in Emma's soul. She heard Scott gasp (although it could just as easily have been her) as Blake leant back from Emma, giving them a brief glimpse of the golden-coloured soul. Although in that moment, Ellie realised that to call it golden belittled what it was. It was golden, sort of, but it wasn't gold—it didn't have that yellowish tinge of jewellery. No, if anything, it was more like a tinted diamond: it sparkled and shimmered. And as it flowed from Emma into Blake, it looked more like a set of twinkling fairy lights than anything else.

Blake slowly rose to his feet, all the while breathing in Emma's soul, and when he was standing, he turned to face Ellie and Scott. Grief was clearly etched into his face, his brow was furrowed, his eyes were filled with unshed tears, and his shoulders were slumped. He looked beaten, and Ellie's heart broke a second time. It was bad enough for her to lose Emma, but how would Blake cope? He'd barely begun to live his life, and now it had been brought to an abrupt end.

Ellie dimly recalled something about Blake being forced to witness every aspect of a person's life when he reaped their soul, and she couldn't help but wonder what Blake saw.

Did he see the time when she, Emma, and Scott had built blanket forts at Grammy and Grandpa Harold's house? They'd absolutely trashed the lounge that day, but oh! What fun they'd had. All of the furniture had been pushed aside so that dining chairs could be strategically place around the room and then they'd draped quilts and throws across the back of the chairs to create a tiny covered over space. Grammy had rustled up some hot chocolate and then she'd squeezed in with them to tell them what they'd assumed were tall tales of a mythical being whose purpose it was to reap the souls of the dying.

Or did he see Emma's first kiss with a boy from school? Of course, Ellie hadn't witnessed that one herself, but she vividly remembered Emma describing it as like having a wet hoover attached to her face. She'd sworn off boys after that, for a while at least.

While Ellie didn't literally see Emma's life flash before her eyes, she couldn't help but recall just some of the many moments that they'd shared together. Everything from the mundane to the major, most of which had been filled with laughter, but some of which had been filled with sorrow. Emma had been such a big part of her life that a gaping hole was being torn into the very fabric of her being, and no doubt it would fester like an ulcerated sore for many years to come.

For a while no one moved, Blake was clearly absorbing what he'd learned, and Ellie was still in shock. She remained nestled in the comforting embrace of Scott, whose whole body was tense. Ellie knew that he was grieving too, Emma was his sister after all. But then Blake stumbled, as if the ground underneath him moved. One minute he was standing perfectly still, and the next he lurched forwards, steadying himself by placing one foot in front of the other and holding his arms out to the sides.

"Blake, what is it? What's wrong?" Ellie asked, taking a small step closer to him, breaking away from the warmth and solidarity offered to her by Scott.

"I don't—" Blake started to answer, but before he could finish his sentence, unseen hands lifted him into the air. His spine was pulled straight and both his arms and legs were snapped tight.

"Blake!" Ellie exclaimed, unconsciously covering her mouth with her hands.

But Blake didn't answer. Instead, a bright light burst forth from his body. It erupted from the top of head, it blazed from his eyes, his ears, and his mouth, and it flared from his hands and feet. Ellie was forced to shield her eyes to ensure that she wasn't blinded by the burning star that Blake had become.

In time, a new voice forced her to look up. "Ellie. Scott."

Where Blake had been standing, a stranger now stood. Ellie rubbed her eyes to make sure that she wasn't seeing things and glanced over her shoulder at Scott. Confusion had twisted his features.

The stranger wasn't as tall as Blake, and he was bulkier, with plain features. His brown hair was cropped short, and he had the beginnings of a beard that was streaked with grey. He was standing exactly where Blake had been, with his legs shoulder width apart and hands clasped loosely in front of him.

Scott found his voice before Ellie did. "Who are you?" he asked, moving to stand beside Ellie so that he could take her hand in his. "And where's Blake?"

"My name is John," the stranger introduced himself. "And I am Blake. Or rather Blake is a part of me."

Ellie gasped, but Scott didn't react. She'd caught on quicker than he had; she'd had longer to absorb the details that Emma and Blake had shared with her over the last few months. "John?" she asked. "But that means…" Her voice trailed off into nothing.

"That's correct, Ellie. I'm Blake's father."

"How is this possible? I mean… it's just so…"

The corners of John's mouth lifted into a barely perceptible smile. "The golden soul is now as it should always have been."

"I don't understand, though. Blake has reaped the soul before, hasn't he? Surely he must have." Ellie's voice rose an octave. "He must have reaped the soul of Emma's ancestors."

"Of course, but he didn't know about the golden soul then. It's true what they say, there's power in knowledge."

"But—"

"Only when Blake met the one he was destined to love could he be made whole again, only with Emma's passing could I be brought back into this world."

"No!" Ellie shook her head. "No! That's not fair." She was openly crying again. "They'd only just found each other. Emma was happy. For the first time in her life, she was really happy. Bring her back. Give them back their souls." Pulling her hand free from Scott's, she used the back of it to wipe her nose.

"Ellie… you don't know what you're asking," John replied.

"I do! I want my friend back. And you can do it, can't you?"

"No, child, I can't." John gently shook his head from side to side. "I can't give Blake and Emma the golden soul back," he finished, before turning to face Seith, who'd barked while John was still speaking, not that Ellie had heard it, but she'd felt it. She'd felt Scott flinch beside her as well. "Bronwyn… my love." John smiled again, but this time his eyes shone with delight.

"Bronwyn?" Scott interrupted. "That's Seith."

"Ah yes! That's the name you've hidden behind for all of these centuries, isn't it, my beloved?"

"Bronwyn?" Ellie repeated. "As in…"

"Yes, as in Emma's great-grandmother, several times removed of course." John directed his answer at Ellie and Scott before turning back to Bronwyn. "You can transform if you want, you know."

Seith—or was it Bronwyn?—only snarled at John in reply.

"Bronwyn." John kept his voice low, attempting to soothe the beast, whose maw remained curled into a vicious-looking grimace. "Yes, I know that he's my son and she's your granddaughter, but what you ask…"

"What?" Ellie butted into the conversation, even though she could only hear what John was saying. "What's she asking you to do?"

Seith barked again.

"I was going to tell them," John answered Seith. "Bronwyn wants me to bring Blake and Emma back to life."

"But you just said that you couldn't do that," Ellie mumbled, her heart leaden in her chest.

"No, I didn't. I said that I couldn't give Blake and Emma the golden soul back. I can give them another soul, though, a normal soul."

"So, do it!" Ellie felt hope flare within her.

"Blake doesn't have a body," Scott remarked, a puzzled look on his face.

"Of course he has a body," John replied. "He just never learned how to keep it on this plane."

"Fantastic!" Ellie beamed.

"It's not quite that easy, child."

"Why not? You've already said that you can do it, you can give Emma and Blake a soul. That means they'll live again, doesn't it?"

"Blake will, yes. But look at Emma. Really look at her body. Her injuries are too grave. She'll only die again."

"But… she…" Ellie stumbled over her words. The rollercoaster of emotions was never-ending. Joy had overwhelmed her when Abaddon had first appeared, but that had quickly turned into an all-consuming grief when Abaddon had said what she'd said. Abaddon… it all seemed to revolve around Abaddon. Ellie turned to Scott, her eyes wide. "Abaddon!" she exclaimed, bouncing on the balls of her feet while clapping her hands together.

"What about Abaddon?" John asked.

"If you bring Emma back to life, Abaddon can heal her. She's healed me before, twice actually." A grin lit up Ellie's face.

"And you think she'll do this for you? Angels aren't always known for being altruistic."

"But I thought angels were the good guys?" Scott said.

John shrugged, a maybe-yes, maybe-no kind of answer.

"She'll do it for me. I know she will," Ellie crowed before looking up towards the ceiling and yelling at the top of her voice. "Abaddon! Abaddon! Get your ass back here before Blake kills me! Abaddon!"

"He wouldn't dare!" Abaddon spat, appearing back in Ellie's apartment between where John was standing at one end of the sofa and where Ellie and Scott were standing at the other. Braced ready for action, she thrust her sword, which was smeared with some kind of black and red residue, towards John, while covering Ellie and Scott with her wings.

"It's nice to see you again, Abaddon." John didn't even flinch as the point of Abaddon's sword was pushed against his chest. "If you wouldn't mind…" He nodded towards where the blade was now resting against his sternum.

"I…" Abaddon let both her sword and her wings fall.

Ellie couldn't stop a snigger from escaping. Abaddon was never lost for words.

"But you…" Abaddon twisted her body to glare at Ellie.

Ellie nodded. "I lied," she confirmed, a smile lighting up her face. "John can bring Emma and Blake back. But you need to heal Emma when he does, or else she'll only die again." The words poured out of her like water from a tap.

Abaddon turned back to face John, the porcelain-like skin on her forehead creased and her mouth shaped into a silent 'o'. "But… I didn't know you could bring people back to life?"

"Not many do."

"Yes, but…"

"But what?" John asked, one eyebrow raised.

"Why haven't you ever raised the dead before?"

"Because people are born to die. It's a part of life."

"So why bring Emma and Blake back?"

"Because they're mine and because I can," John stated, a hard edge creeping into his voice for the first time since he'd returned into being. "And because after everything they've been through," his voice was softer now, "they deserve a chance at happiness, do they not?" He tilted his head to one side, clearly waiting for an answer.

Chapter 22 – Ellie
Tuesday 4th June 2019

Ellie held her breath, waiting for Abaddon to answer. She'd been so certain that Abaddon would heal Emma, but what if she wouldn't? Or couldn't? Abaddon had healed Ellie twice now, but each time it had only been a minor cut. Emma had been tortured. Not only that, but the golden soul had been killing her from the inside out. And what if Abaddon had only been able to heal Ellie because of their connection? Because Abaddon's blood ran through her veins? No, that couldn't be true; she'd been able to help Scott *see* even though he didn't have angel blood in his veins, so she'd be able to heal Emma. She had to; the alternative was simply unbearable.

"Well?" John asked. Neither Ellie nor Scott had moved during the exchange. Ellie didn't know about Scott, but she hadn't dared.

Abaddon arched her eyebrows. "What's in it for me?" she asked, casually folding her arms across the front of her body.

"Abaddon!" Ellie hissed.

"What?" Abaddon asked, unfolding her arms so that she could flick her hair over her shoulder.

"Are you really bargaining for Emma's life right now?"

"It's okay, Ellie," John intervened. "Just exactly what is it that you want, Abaddon?"

"Well… you could open the portal into Heaven so that all of angel-kind can live out their lives on Earth."

"No, Abaddon. I can't do that."

"Why not?"

"Because there needs to be balance here on Earth. I know that now."

Abaddon rolled her eyes. "You could open the portal into *both* Heaven and Hell then."

"So that both sides would be evenly matched?" John raised an eyebrow.

"Exactly!" Abaddon nodded enthusiastically, a broad smile

lighting up her face.

"No, Abaddon, I can't do that either. You'd turn Earth into a battleground, and mankind would be slaughtered."

Abaddon's face fell. "Well, what can you do?"

"I can open the portal for you so that you can go back to Heaven if you want." Abaddon wrinkled her nose in disgust. "Or I open the portal and bring a limited number of your friends to Earth."

"How many?" Abaddon asked, her voice a little brighter, her shoulders a little squarer.

"We'll discuss that another time, when the children aren't listening," John said, breaking eye contact with Abaddon to glance at Ellie and Scott. "Now then, do we have a deal?" He held his hand out to Abaddon.

A silence engulfed the room. Ellie held her breath once more, until eventually Abaddon reached out and took John's hand in hers. "We have a deal," she confirmed.

"Thank God for that," Ellie muttered.

"Don't thank God." Abaddon glanced over her shoulder, looking every inch the angelic being that she was. "Thank me…" she declared, patting herself on the chest before pulling a face. "And maybe John," she admitted, although her admission was said much more quietly.

"How does this work then?" Ellie ignored Abaddon.

John looked over at Ellie and stared hard. "Ellie, this is a one-time offer, you know that, don't you?"

"Of course I do."

"I won't be bringing your parents back when they die."

"No, I know that."

"Or you."

"What do you mean, or me?"

"I sense that you have quite the life ahead of you. You need to be careful because I will not be bringing anyone else back to life, not even you."

"Nothing's going to happen to Ellie," Scott declared fiercely, draping his arm over Ellie's shoulder and hugging her into him.

"It might not," John agreed. "But if it does, I will not do for her what I'm about to do for Emma and Blake."

"Fine, that's fine," Ellie replied, while Scott asked, "Why not?"

"Because Ellie will have a choice in how she lives her life. Emma and Blake didn't."

"Honestly, it's fine, Scott. I'm fine. Nothing's going to happen to me."

Scott continued to frown, but eventually he nodded his head. John looked at Abaddon. "Are you ready?"

"Yes."

"You'll need to act as soon as Emma starts to breathe again."

"Yeah, yeah, whatever," Abaddon said, absently inspecting her nails. They were perfectly manicured despite the fact that she still wore her armour. Each was painted pink with a crisp white tip.

"If you wouldn't mind…" John's eyes bored into Abaddon, who sighed melodramatically before disappearing with a huff. When she reappeared, at the head of the sofa, Abaddon the angel had left the building. Instead, Abaddon looked like a well-endowed, middle-aged woman, with long hair curled into ringlets. She had dark brown eyes and was heavily made-up.

Scott gasped out loud.

"What?" Abaddon asked, giggling.

"Don't you think that's a bit inappropriate?" Ellie asked, bumping Scott with her hip at the same time. Abaddon was wearing a low-cut white top that clung to her ample bust, revealing the edges of a black lacy bra.

"Not for where I'm going next, no. A good battle always makes me… well, let's just say that it gets me in the mood." Abaddon smiled.

Ellie rolled her eyes.

"You might want to back up a little," John said to Ellie and Scott, but he didn't give them time to move before reaching into the ether and pulling Blake's body from it. He did it so casually that one minute the space in front of the sofa was empty and the next, Ellie and Scott were forced to retreat.

"Blake!" Ellie gasped, automatically covering her mouth with her hands. Blake's body looked like a waxwork figurine. His skin was a bluish grey and slack around his face, and his eyes looked like a pair of glass beads.

"Bloody hell," Scott muttered, taking another step backwards, pulling Ellie with him.

John ignored both Ellie and Scott. He knelt on the floor at the head of Blake's body and placed his hands, one each, on Blake's temples. Gently, he tilted Blake's head backwards towards him and then he leant forwards, covering Blake's mouth with his own before breathing out. It was almost as though he was giving mouth-to-mouth, but without the chest compressions.

Ellie watched as Blake's chest rose and fell, once, twice, and then a third time. "It's not working," she mumbled, her voice sounding out of place in the hush that had descended.

John continued what he was doing, and Blake's chest rose again. This time his body twitched. His fingers curled into a fist, and one of his feet spasmed. John stopped breathing for Blake, and instead started blowing on him. He leant back from Blake's body but continued to blow. A silvery substance flowed from John's mouth into Blake's. It sparkled and shimmered in the light of Ellie's apartment, joyfully dancing between the two men until it was fully absorbed into Blake.

Blake coughed weakly before filling his lungs with air. His breathing was ragged, but he was breathing on his own. John had done it; he'd brought Blake back to life. It truly was a miracle.

Blake's breathing slowly returned to normal. He pulled himself into a seated position, turning his body so that he could lean his back against the sofa. "Ellie… Scott…" he said, glancing in their direction. "What… where…?" He blinked and turned his head. "Who are you?" he asked, now looking at John, who was still kneeling on the floor.

"My son," John whispered, tears streaming openly down his face.

"I don't…" Blake closed his eyes and shook his head.

To Ellie, it looked like he was trying to clear away the fog that must have descended when he'd ceased to exist, when the golden soul had fused together and recreated John. "Blake, it's—"

"Emma!" Blake exclaimed, jerking upright. He scrambled to turn towards the sofa. His movements were uncoordinated, but eventually he ended up on his knees facing Emma's body. "Emma," he sobbed, taking hold of her hands in his. "Why?"

"She'll be fine, Blake."

"How can you say that? She's dead. I reaped her soul…. Oh my God," Blake stumbled backwards, letting Emma's hands fall back onto her stomach. "I reaped her soul." The look of horror on his face told Ellie all that she needed to know. Guilt was eating away at Blake, gnawing on his innards.

"My son..." John kept his voice low. "You did what needed to be done. It was your duty to reap all souls, including Emma's, and in doing so, you brought the golden soul back together again. You gave me back my life."

"No, I shouldn't have. I..." Blake broke down and cried.

Before Ellie had time to move, before she could offer Blake any comfort, Seith was there. She—because Ellie now knew Seith was really Bronwyn—leapt the sofa in one easy bound and rested her muzzle on Blake's shoulder. Blake took the comfort on offer and wrapped his arms around the beast.

"Do you think we could get on with it?" Abaddon interrupted. "Touching as this is, I do have other things to do, you know?"

"Abaddon! Really?" Ellie glared at her.

"It's okay, Ellie. Blake needs Emma. As Abaddon so delicately pointed out, I should get on with it. Are you ready, Abaddon?"

"I've been ready for the last fifteen minutes," Abaddon muttered, "ever since you last asked me if I was ready."

John nodded his head, accepting Abaddon's criticism without comment, and started the process of bringing Emma back to life.

Chapter 23 – Emma
Tuesday 4th June 2019

Pain had swallowed me whole. Not only that, but it insisted on gnawing on my bones, as if I hadn't suffered enough already. Every muscle ached. Every nerve ending was alive. And don't get me started on the searing agony that was my stomach. Someone was having a whale of a time with a pair of white-hot pokers and my kidneys, or was it my liver?

Damn it! I thought. After everything I'd done, after all the torture I'd borne, I kind of thought I deserved to be in Heaven. How had I ended up in Hell? I mean, come on! I'd saved the world, hadn't I?

Think, Emma, think! The last thing I remembered was Blake. He'd come to me despite the fact that I'd tried to stop him. And then… what had happened after that? Oh yes! Terrance and his cronies had started chanting, some weird biblical crap that meant nothing to me. It had been soothing in a funny kind of way, and I'd found myself wanting to listen to it, to try and understand its meaning, but Johnna had made me ignore it so that I could… what had I done? Oh, damn and blast… that's what I'd done. Once upon a time, I'd promised Blake that I'd never command him to do anything ever again, but I'd had to. I'd had to command him to close the portal. If I hadn't done it, then demons would be walking about freely on Earth already. And more than that, Blake would be dead. I couldn't bear the thought of him being dead.

If I had to suffer an eternity of agony to ensure Blake's well-being, I'd do it and then some. Idly I wondered what would happen to him now. My soul would be reborn in due course so he had a chance at some kind of life. Mind you… if my soul was reborn, that would give the demons another opportunity at opening the portal. Crap basket! Had it all been for nothing? I had to warn someone, anyone.

I tried to move, to sit up, but all I succeeded in doing was flopping around like a fish out of water, and if I could barely sit up, what chance did I have of warning someone about the demons? I needed to get back home, but how? I was dead, which meant that the only way back for me was as a ghost. Maybe I was a ghost already because if Blake reaped everyone's soul, then no one went to Heaven or Hell. If that was the case, though, why did I hurt so much?

Blake had explained how ghosts came into being once upon a time. He'd said something about a person's spirit remaining behind when their body died and he reaped their soul. But that wasn't possible for me; my spirit would have fused with my soul, just like Johnna's had done, because the golden soul was unchanging. No, wait! That was it! I wasn't in Hell; I was with Johnna.

Johnna? I called, peering into the gloom. Wherever I was, it was pitch black. *Johnna?* I said again. *Anyone?* No one answered, but in the distance, I thought I saw a pinprick of light. *Hello?* Still no one answered, but the speck of light grew brighter. It cast an orange glow that crept closer and closer to my body until eventually it washed over me.

Oh joy, what fresh hell is this? I wondered. Everywhere the light touched, my skin felt like it was being scorched by the heat of a thousand suns. The only advantage being that all of my individual aches and pains were chased away by the fire as it consumed me whole.

Seconds turned into minutes. Minutes turned into hours. And then, when I couldn't stand it any longer, I screamed.

"Emma?" Someone said my name. Who was that? It didn't sound like Johnna.

"Emma? Come on, you can do it." Someone else was talking to me, imploring me to wake up, but that wasn't possible. I was dead, wasn't I? I mean, I was conscious, but I was also dead. My eyes were already open, weren't they?

The feeling of being set alight slowly dimmed, and I heaved a sigh of relief.

"She's coming around. Oh, thank God for that."

Ellie? I thought. That certainly sounded like Ellie, but as far as I knew, Ellie was still alive. Although Terrance had gloated about having both her and Scott ready and waiting to be served up as dinner to the King of Hell. Tears escaped from between my eyes, and without thinking, I reached up to brush them away. *They're closed! My eyes are closed, but... how...*

"Emma? Please, I need you."

Blake? Evidently my mind was playing tricks on me because Blake couldn't possibly be wherever I was. If he had been, I'd be drowning in his emotions. To be honest, knowing Blake as I did, I'd be suffocated by his guilt.

"Nnargh," I mumbled.

"Yes! Come on, Emma."

Now that was odd. I'd spoken aloud for the first time since waking up and someone had answered. Maybe I wasn't dead. But… no, that wasn't possible. I was definitely dead. I'd worked as a vet nurse for many years. I knew basic anatomy, and my injuries were too severe for me to have survived.

"Emma!" Someone snapped, although judging from the hand that was now stroking my cheek, whoever was with me wasn't actually vexed, just desperate. Yes, that's what I heard in their voice, desperation.

Curiosity got the better of me, and I pried my eyelids apart, only to find that the light was too bright. I squeezed my eyes closed again, but as I did so, a single image remained seared on my brain.

"Blake?" I croaked, forcing my eyes back open.

"Emma." It was Blake! Relief was written all over his face. I was alive! But why wasn't I feeling his emotions?

Blake? I asked silently. He didn't answer, but he did pull me into his arms. I expected to feel tentacles of pain grappling with my body but nope… nothing. I felt better than I had done in a long time. Tentatively, I wrapped my arms around Blake and squeezed. Nothing hurt! What…?

"Emma," Blake said, breathing heavily in my ear. "I thought I'd lost you."

"I don't…" My voice trailed off into nothing. I wanted to say that I didn't understand, but I couldn't get the words out. My wits were too scrambled.

Blake released his hold and helped me into a seated position. And then I was crushed under the weight of Seith.

"Seith! You're… real!" I exclaimed, not knowing how else to explain away the fact that I was hugging Blake's guardian. The coarse feel of fur under my hand certainly felt real, but before I could process the feeling and wonder how it was possible for a spectral beast to be corporeal all of a sudden, Seith was pushed aside and Ellie was pulling me to my feet. She and Scott enveloped me in their combined embrace.

"What's going on?" I asked, still caught up in Ellie's and Scott's arms.

"Emma, you were dead!" Ellie choked out the words.

"John saved you," Scott added.

"John? Who's John?" I asked, pulling away from the pair of them. A feeling of nausea washed over me, and I swayed on my own two feet, but Blake was there. He pulled me onto his lap, tucking me into the protective warmth of his body, making me feel wonderfully petite.

Thank you, I whispered silently to him.

Scott mirrored Blake, sitting at the opposite end of the sofa, with Ellie on his lap, and Seith sat in front of us. I glanced around them all, only then realising that we were in Ellie's apartment, and we were not alone. Two strangers stood staring at me.

How did I get here? I asked silently. "Who are you?" I asked out loud, wondering why Blake wasn't answering my first question.

The curly-haired woman spoke up first. "Emma, it's nice to meet you at last." She nodded in my direction. "You can thank me later," she continued. "I'm outta here," she finished with a toss of her head, and then literally disappeared.

I couldn't help the gasp that escaped my lips. "Who was that?"

Ellie giggled before answering. "That," she stressed, "was Abaddon. She's probably gone to hook up with someone."

"Ellie," Scott reprimanded.

"What?" Ellie asked, the picture of innocence. "It's true."

"Yes, but she has just saved Emma's life."

"And I," the man interrupted, cutting across Ellie and Scott and stepping forwards to offer me his hand, "am John. But you know that already, don't you?" He smiled warmly while I shook his hand. His skin was warm against my own.

"John..." I mumbled, my eyes never leaving his face. And then it dawned on me who he was. "John!" I exclaimed, releasing his hand. "But, how?"

John stood up straight. "When Blake reaped your soul, I was reborn."

"I... erm... how...?" I glanced at Blake and then back at John.

"Ah yes, that. Long story short, I brought you both back to life, and Abaddon healed your injuries so that you could live again."

"But wouldn't that mean...?"

"No, you and Blake no longer share the golden soul. That's mine, and this time I'm going to keep it. Or at least I will if this one ever deigns to forgive me." He nodded in the direction of Seith.

"Seith?"

"Actually," Ellie reached across and placed her hand on my leg, "that's Bronwyn."

"Bronwyn? As in…?"

"Yes." Ellie nodded, her eyes sparkling with delight. She took her hand back and reached up to pat Scott's cheek before continuing. "So now everyone gets to have a happy ending."

Seith—Bronwyn—didn't look so sure about that. She pointed her nose up towards the ceiling, her head turned to one side. It looked like she was in a huff.

"Bronwyn, please," John begged. "I only did it to give you a child."

Bronwyn whipped her head in John's direction, her eyes narrowed into dark slits.

"I love you," John continued. "I've only ever loved you."

Bronwyn continued to stare, but between one breath and the next, she started to transform. Her muzzle shortened and her back straightened while her hind legs lengthened. Soon, it actually was Bronwyn who stood in front of us, and not Seith. All trace of Seith's trademark black fur with its green highlights were gone. Instead, a beautiful woman with long copper hair stood in front of us. She had hazel-coloured eyes and milky white skin, lots of milky white skin because she was as naked as the day was long.

"Our daughters have suffered through the centuries because of you," she spat, placing her hands on her hips. Clearly, her nudity didn't bother her, although I was having trouble knowing where to look.

"I didn't know that would happen." John stripped off his jacket and offered it to Bronwyn, who snatched it from his hand.

"And your son," Bronwyn continued, flipping the jacket over her shoulders and sliding her arms into it. "For nearly a thousand years, he's grieved for a life that he couldn't have."

"I know." John hung his head in shame. "And I'm sorry. I just wanted you to have what your heart desired."

"I wanted you." Bronwyn finished, buttoning up John's jacket before folding her arms across her body.

"You broke it off with me." John's eyes flashed with defiance.

"I just needed time."

"But I didn't know that... did I?"

"If I may," Ellie interrupted politely. "Can we skip to the part where you two make up? I've got questions."

"Ellie!" Scott squeezed her into him.

"No, I'm with Ellie," I said, twisting on Blake's lap to face Scott. "I've got questions too. Isn't Blake the Keeper of Souls anymore?" I turned back to John. "How come Bronwyn can transform at will? Blake's only ever whole near me." I phrased my question purposely to annoy Blake, wanting to feel a spike of irritation. Scott glared at me, but I got nothing from Blake other than a slight squeeze. "What?" I asked, shrugging my shoulders, puzzled by the lack of a reaction from Blake. Maybe the fact that I'd died had softened him? "They're obviously still in love. Look at them." I nodded my head at John and Bronwyn, who'd edged closer together.

"I like their plan," John said, smiling at Bronwyn. "We were both at fault."

Bronwyn sniffed. "Answer Emma's questions," she commanded, her arms still crossed over her body.

"Whatever you want, my darling." John held Bronwyn's gaze for a moment before looking at me. "No, Emma, Blake is not the Keeper of Souls anymore. You're both normal people with normal souls, and barring accident or injury, you should both live long and happy lives before dying of old age. Was there anything else you wanted to know?"

"Well, you didn't answer my question about Bronwyn, and how did she end up as Seith anyway?"

"Ah, that." John glanced back at Bronwyn. "Do you want to tell them, or shall I?"

Bronwyn only stared at John.

"I guess I'll tell them then." John paused before continuing, "That was God's doing. He wanted someone to keep an eye on Blake, so he offered Bronwyn the chance to become his guardian on her death. There was a catch though; she couldn't tell Blake anything that I'd done. God believed He was punishing me for my actions, instead He was punishing my son." John bowed his head for a moment, before turning so that he could face Bronwyn square on. "Happy?" he asked.

"And?" Bronwyn prompted.

"And what?"

"You've still not answered Emma's first question about me."

"Shouldn't you answer that one yourself, darling?"

Bronwyn raised an eyebrow, but she did answer the question. "Blake couldn't materialise on his own because you had half of his soul, Emma. You were the Key to unlocking Blake's power."

My jaw dropped. I'd been the reason that Blake had suffered for all of those years. Because of me, he'd missed out on so much. He'd never been able to connect with anyone until he'd met me; he'd never been able to touch anything, let alone taste anything. He hadn't been able to smell perfume or… oh my goodness, he'd missed out on the smell of freshly baked bread, and I was to blame. *Or not,* I thought, pulling myself up short. I hadn't chosen this life for either of us, so why was I blaming myself. If anyone was to blame, it was John.

"I…" I started to say.

"None of it was your fault, Emma," Blake whispered into my ear. It was almost like he'd been able to read my mind still, but he'd not heard my last thought. Maybe he could just read me now?

"Well? Am I forgiven?" John asked, not speaking to me anymore.

"I suppose," Bronwyn finally admitted before flinging her arms around John's neck and rubbing her nose against his. "I love you too," she whispered, barely loud enough for me to hear, and then she placed her lips gently on his.

Chapter 24 – Emma
Sunday 8th September 2019

"Oh, Ellie!" I couldn't help myself. She looked beautiful, like a sun-kissed goddess who'd been blessed by the fae folk themselves.

"Do you like it?" Ellie asked, glancing briefly over her shoulder to look at me before turning back to the full-length mirror so she could gaze at her reflection some more.

"You know I do. You look stunning! Absolutely beautiful."

Ellie didn't answer, but her smile would have melted the ice caps if she'd been standing at the North Pole.

Of course, I'd seen Ellie's dress before. I'd been there when she'd first tried it on. I'd been there for every single one of her fittings—and there had been a few. And I'd helped her into it only moments before. But seeing her in it, with all of her hair and makeup done… well, that was something else. She looked radiant.

"Is it time?" Ellie asked, finally turning to face me.

"Not quite, but everyone's here. Your dad says he'll come and knock for us when they're ready."

"Okay." Ellie grinned. "I can't believe it's finally happening. I'm so excited. Soon I'll be Mrs. Ellie Moore."

"You will indeed. There's still time if you want to leg it, you know?" I couldn't help it. My dry sense of humour just wouldn't pipe down lately. The only logical explanation was that I was going crazy. Or else it was the aftereffects of everything that I'd been through. It was finally over; I was finally free to get on with my life, but only after I'd seen Ellie safely down the aisle.

"Emma!"

"What?" I feigned surprise. "All I'm saying is that it's Scott. As in my big brother. Do you really want to tie yourself to him for the rest of your life?"

Ellie rolled her eyes, but the smile remained firmly fixed on her face. "I do…. I really do. I love him so much."

"Hmmm." I took a seat on the edge of the bed. "Well, as long as you're sure? I'll cover for you if you've changed your mind though. You did save my life after all. It's the least I can do."

"Actually, it was Scott who saved your life really. He was the one who figured out that the runes were all linked."

"Be that as it may, you led the charge, and it was your blood that deactivated the runes."

"But—"

"No buts, Ellie. The prophecy was about you."

"I still don't really get that. You closed the portal all by yourself."

"Maybe." I shrugged. I hadn't really closed the portal all by myself; I'd had help from my ancestors, but I knew what Ellie meant: there had been no one else physically present. "But if you'd have done what Abaddon originally wanted you to do, I wouldn't have been alive to close the portal."

"So?"

"So… my soul would have been reborn. The demons would have been able to perform the ritual using the next child to carry the golden soul, and I doubt that a baby would have been able to do what I did." I paused. "Urgh, that sounds conceited," I added, wrinkling my nose.

Ellie laughed. "It does sound conceited, and you're wrong. Your soul wouldn't have been reborn because John was always going to reappear when Blake reaped your soul."

"Huh." I tilted my head, thinking it through. Why had Ellie been so important, then? Even Johnna had been insistent that it was 'up to Ellie.' "I don't know. I can only assume that you breaking and entering was critical somehow. I mean, if you hadn't deactivated the runes when you did, Terrance would have started the ritual for a second time."

"Maybe. But you'd have stopped him again."

I wrinkled my nose. "I don't know about that. I kind of killed myself stopping him the first time around."

"No, Terrance killed you."

"You mean Matthew killed me."

"No, it was Terrance. Matthew wouldn't have stabbed you without Terrance making him."

I didn't know what to say to that because in a way Ellie was right, but I still didn't know how I felt about Matthew. He'd survived that night—an angel had relocated him in much the same way that Abaddon had relocated Ellie and Scott and then me and Blake—and I *was* glad about that because he had been kind to me all the while I'd been held captive. In a very weird and twisted way, you could even say that he'd looked after me. But he'd also abducted me in the first place and, even if Terrance had made him, he *had* been the one to stab me. In the end, I opted for changing the subject. "Well, let's discuss that another day," I declared, standing up from my perch. "Now then, let me check you over."

If she weren't my best friend, I'd have been jealous of how amazing she looked. The sleeveless bodice hugged her figure, and the dress' sweetheart neckline and dropped waist suited Ellie's petite frame perfectly. It was the perfect shade of white, with a yellow tulle overlay that was so delicate, the colour was almost imperceptible. It made Ellie look like she was standing in a beam of light, or like she'd been kissed by angels—which she had. It had a relatively small train because, let's be honest, if she'd opted for a longer train, the dress would have worn her rather than the other way around.

"Turn around," I instructed.

Ellie dutifully obliged so that I could check that every single one of the tiny buttons cascading down the back of her dress had been properly done up.

"Turn again," I said when I was satisfied that nothing was out of place.

Again, Ellie complied. She'd chosen to keep her hair and makeup quite simple. Her hair was pinned into a bun at the nape of her neck, and she'd accentuated her natural beauty with neutral-coloured eye makeup and a coral lipstick.

"Perfect," I whispered, a lump forming in the back of my throat. "You really do look perfect."

"Hey!" Ellie snapped. "Don't you dare cry, not yet anyway. If you cry, then I'll cry, and neither one of us can afford for our mascara to run right now."

I laughed because... well... what else could I do? And then we were hugging. Ellie wasn't just my best friend; she was so much more than that. She'd been a part of my life since forever, since we'd both been in nappies. She knew everything about me—she'd been with me from the very beginning. Heck, she'd broken into a demon-infested mansion for me.

"If I may…" Frank, Ellie's Dad, interrupted. "I knocked, but you obviously didn't hear me."

Ellie and I both turned to look at Frank. He wore a dark grey morning suit, complete with a purple waistcoat that matched my dress, and on his lapel, he had a buttonhole that consisted of a single yellow rose next to a tiny spray of baby's breath, backed by a bright green glossy leaf.

"Ellie… my darling… you look sublime."

"Thank you, Daddy." Ellie beamed at him.

"And you look lovely as well, Emma." Frank smiled at me.

"Thanks, Frank." Naturally, my dress wasn't in the same league as Ellie's, but it was beautiful. Like Ellie's, it had a fitted bodice and a sweetheart neckline, but unlike Ellie's, mine didn't have a tulle overlay and it flared out from just above (rather than just below) my waist. And of course, it wasn't white! Mine was aubergine, so dark that it was almost black.

"Well then, ladies. Are you ready?" Frank held out his hand for Ellie.

"One second, we just need the flowers," I replied, while Ellie ignored her father's hand in favour of a hug.

Along with everything else that the maid of honour usually does, because of my love of gardening, I'd been put in charge of the flowers. Everything from buttonholes to table centres had been part of my remit. I didn't actually create anything, mind you. Oh no, I left the hard work to the professionals, but I worked with the florist—Charlotte's mum—to design each piece. Ellie's bouquet was a mix of yellow roses, Peruvian lilies, and goldenrods, with some baby's breath and trailing jasmine to soften the edges. The mix of yellows complemented Ellie's dress perfectly. Mine was similar to Ellie's, but the Peruvian lilies had been swapped out for sword lilies that Charlotte's mum had dyed to match my dress.

"Here you go." I held Ellie's bouquet out for her. "We'd best go."

"Are we sufficiently late?" Ellie asked, looking first at Frank and then at me.

"Well, you were supposed to get married at four, and it's now twenty past so I'd say that yes, you're sufficiently late," Frank answered before I could.

"It's not like we have far to go, is it?" Ellie beamed.

Ellie and Scott had chosen to have their wedding in a hotel in the Lake District. It was the perfect setting; the hotel was tucked away out of sight from the main roads so that every window looked out over the beautiful countryside. The advantage of Ellie and Scott having decided on a hotel wedding, in my humble opinion, was that Ellie and I had been able to get ready on-site. We'd spent the morning in the hotel's spa, having facials, manicures, and pedicures, all the while giggling like little school children about everything and nothing while sipping champagne from delicate flute-like glasses. And then we'd retired to the honeymoon suite to get showered and dressed. From there, all we needed to do was descend the most beautiful wooden staircase and walk down a short corridor to the 'manager's office,' which is where Ellie and Scott would officially be united as husband and wife.

The 'manager's office' was a small room with picture windows overlooking one of the lesser-known lakes in the Lake District. Immediately in front of the window, the registrar's table had been placed at a jaunty angle, and in front of that, thirty chairs, each covered with a pale-yellow sash, had been laid out in five rows of six, three each on either side of the room so as to form an aisle.

Ellie, escorted by Frank, walked down the aisle to an instrumental version of Ed Sheeran's 'Photograph.' As soon as she appeared in the doorway, my brother welled up. Like me, he was a redhead, and redheads do not look good when they cry. He fought back the tears, his face growing increasingly scarlet, until Ellie was about halfway down the aisle, and then he gave in.

Of course, I barely glanced at Scott because I only had eyes for Blake. My handsome, my very human, Blake. I'd been a little surprised when Scott had asked Blake to be his best man; they hadn't known each other all that long, but as Scott had said, only the four of us knew what we'd really been through to have our happy ever afters. It seemed only right that the four of us made up the wedding party. Besides which, Scott was a bit of a loner; he didn't really have many other friends. I wasn't the only one in the family who could be hard work! Okay, okay, scratch that. He'd been pining for Ellie for so long that no one else had gotten a look in.

With my eyes on Blake, I followed Ellie down the aisle and took my seat on the left-hand hand side of the room, next to my dad, who was sitting next to my mum.

The ceremony passed in a bit of a blur for me. One minute, the celebrant was welcoming us to the wedding of Ellie and Scott, and the next, Ellie and Scott were sharing their first kiss as newlyweds. Before I knew it, I was on the terrace with Blake, a glass of champagne in one hand and a canapé in the other.

Everyone I loved was nearby: Blake, Ellie and Scott, Mum and Dad, Joanne and Frank, Andrew and Marie, most of the staff from Cedar's… even Mrs. Porter had joined us. Matthew had not been invited. I'd not seen him since… well, since he'd stabbed me. He'd left Cedar's, his official story being that in the wake of his father's death he needed some time out. I didn't know if that was true or if he was up to something else, but it must have been hard for him when everything came out.

After John had resurrected me, I'd rung Mum and Dad, who'd turned up at Ellie's only thirty minutes later, even though that journey should have taken much longer, and then I'd rung the police. I'd told them what had happened, omitting certain details that couldn't be explained away and saying only that whoever had rescued me had dumped me back at Ellie's. I never mentioned Matthew's involvement, but the police learned that Matthew's father was one of my kidnappers. Danny, the policeman who I'd dealt with in the past, said that the theory was Terrance had seen me with Matthew one time and become fixated. Obviously I knew that was a load of rubbish, but I couldn't come up with any other explanation for why someone I'd never met would snatch me away.

Before my thoughts could turn any darker, Joanne interrupted. "Emma," she exclaimed, her eyes sparkling with delight. "You look beautiful." She opened her arms to me, and without hesitation, I stepped into Joanne's embrace.

"Thank you, Joanne, you do too," I said, squeezing her tightly.

"I'm glad everything turned out the way it did," she whispered into my ear.

"I know you are." I smiled and let my arms drop to create space for Blake.

"Blake," Joanne acknowledged with a nod of her head. She took a small step backwards so that the three of us could talk.

"Joanne," Blake replied.

"Do you think you'll ever forgive me, Blake?" Joanne asked, her smile dying.

"No."

"I am sorry, you know."

"I know you are."

"But you won't forgive me?"

"No." Blake paused before adding, "But I'm trying to get past it, for Emma's sake."

Joanne's smile returned, although it wasn't quite as bright as it had been. "Thank you, Blake. I appreciate that."

I'd purposely stayed quiet while Blake and Joanne talked because, while I understood Blake's position, I'd chosen to forgive Joanne. Yes, she'd tried to kill me, but she'd done it with the best of intentions. Besides which, I'd met pure evil since then, so what was a little attempted murder between friends?

Chapter 25 – Blake
Tuesday 25th February 2020

Emma's cries of pure agony drove hard shafts of pain through Blake's core. The worst of it being that there was literally nothing he could do to ease her burden.

"Push, Emma," the doctor barked.

Emma cried out once more, bearing down with her whole body while also crushing Blake's hands in her own. She was propped up on a hospital bed, with her legs held up on one side by a nurse and on the other by Ellie. Blake thought the whole thing looked barbaric, but when he'd commented on it, Emma had shot him a look full of pure venom. At that point, she'd been having contractions for several hours though.

Sweat poured from her forehead as she pushed again.

"That's it. One more and I think she'll be out. Good girl, keep going," the doctor encouraged. "Sir, if you want to see your little girl being born, you might want to come here."

Blake looked at the doctor, glanced briefly at Emma, and then repositioned himself so that he could see over Emma's knees. He was just in time to witness his baby's head crowning.

"Oh, Emma!" Tears welled up in Blake's eyes.

"Push, Emma!" the doctor commanded, and Emma did just that, her face turning scarlet. Once, twice, and then the sweet sound of a baby wailing filled the room.

"Do you want to cut the cord?" the doctor asked, looking at Blake.

Did he? Blake wanted to do everything that he could, and more. He'd been over the moon when Emma had handed him a pregnancy test. He cried tears of joy when he'd felt the baby move for the first time. And now, he was finally a father.

Blake took the scissors that the doctor offered him and tentatively placed them around the baby's cord. As he cut through the spongy material, he gazed at his little girl. She had a mop of thick dark hair, chubby little cheeks, and the most delicate eyelashes that he'd ever seen. Blake's world turned upside down and inside out in an instant. A feeling of love washed over him. "You've done it, Emma," he said, looking up at her. "We have a beautiful baby girl."

"You do indeed, sir," one of the nurses remarked. "What are you going to call her?"

Blake smiled at Emma. "Her name is Johnna Elizabeth Moore."

Epilogue
Monday 31st August 2020

"Again!" Abaddon barked.

"I can't." Ellie collapsed on the floor and rolled onto her back. "I can't go again."

"You have to."

"No, please don't make me." Ellie was sweating profusely.

"The demons will not give you time to catch your breath." Abaddon poked Ellie's thigh with her toe.

"I know, I know. But everything hurts."

"Oh for God's sake, give me your hand."

Ellie lifted her arm up, but otherwise remained still, forcing Abaddon to take her hand and hold its weight. An orange glow lit up the air. "Better?" Abaddon asked, releasing Ellie's hand.

"Much." Ellie pulled herself into a sitting position.

Abaddon sat down next to her. "If you're serious about doing this, then you need to train harder."

"I know. I will," she replied, staring into the corner of the room where a black and tan dog lay on the ground. "Come here, girl." She opened her arms to the dog that she'd first met in the demon house.

Abaddon ignored the dog as it rose and trotted over to Ellie. "You don't have to do this, you know. No one is making you."

Ellie didn't answer at first; she was too busy giving the dog kisses. "I know that too," she eventually said, "but I want to. I want to use the gifts that you gave me."

"There are other ways to use your gifts."

"No. Whether you like it or not, I am going to hunt down and kill the demons who tortured my best friend."

The End. Well, it's the end of Emma's story at least, but Ellie might yet be back.

A WORD FROM THE AUTHOR

If you enjoyed *A Grim Ending*, why don't you follow me on Instagram? I use Instagram to share my life as an author and to post updates about forthcoming events/publications.

I'd also ask that you take 5-10 minutes to leave me a review on your preferred platform. Reviews will not only help me to build my credibility, they will also encourage other readers to pick up my work. You don't need to write *War and Peace*; a simple 'I liked it' will do. Thank you in advance.

My Instagram handle is: rachel21stanley

WHAT'S IN A NAME?
(IN ALPHABETICAL ORDER)

Blake
There are several reported meanings for the name Blake. It can be taken to mean 'dark, with fair skin or hair,' or it can be taken to mean 'very dark or very light' or 'mysteriously incredible,' depending on where it's derived from. As an English surname, it's a derivative of black, which means 'dark,' or a derivative of the old English word *blac*, which means 'pale or fair,' hence the contradictory nature of the name. It is believed to be associated with people who are reserved (I think you'll all agree that Blake is most definitely reserved!), inquisitive, and tender.

Ellie
The literal translation of Ellie is 'bright, shining one' or 'shining light,' as you will know, having read *A Grim Ending*. Alternatively, it can be taken to mean 'beautiful woman.' It was originally a nickname derived from names starting with El—, such as Eleanor or Elizabeth. However, it's increasingly used as a name in its own right. It's usually associated with people who are warm and friendly, which describes Ellie perfectly, in my opinion.

Emma
Emma has its roots in an old Germanic word meaning 'whole' or 'universal,' which, bearing in mind Emma is Blake's whole world, feels about right. Emma is also associated with King Yama, the Lord of the Dead, who is found in Chinese, Japanese, Hindu, Buddhist, and Indian cultures. He is the one who decides if you go to Heaven or to Hell. He's a wrathful God, and while Emma is not wrathful, it won't have escaped your notice that she has a bit of a temper!

Seith
Seith is a Welsh name meaning 'seven.' It's thought that people with the name Seith tend towards shyness and therefore have a tendency to hide

their thoughts. They're spiritual and enjoy time on their own, all of which sounds like Seith. However, Seith was based on the Cu'Sith, which is a Scottish belief. Cu'Sith are huge hounds with green fur. They're silent creatures unless they're hunting. At the start of a hunt, each Cu'Sith barks three times. It's said that if you're not in a safe place before the moment that the final, ear-splitting bark fades away, the Cu'Sith would come for your soul.

Printed in Great Britain
by Amazon